PASSENGER X

Shelena Shorts

Lands Atlantic PUBLISHING

Passenger X
Published through Lands Atlantic Publishing
www.landsatlantic.com

All rights reserved Copyright © 2020 by Shelena Shorts
ISBN: 978-0-9971551-4-3

PASSENGER X

Shelena Shorts

Lands Atlantic PUBLISHING

Acknowledgments

Here we are with my 7th novel! It's amazing that you can be anywhere, and you are here, so thank YOU! Let's do this! Without you, I'd just be reading this myself and what fun would that be for these characters?!

I also want to thank my dear mother so very much for taking this publishing journey with me 10 years ago. You are a fantastic editor and I love working with you. Dawn Morton, your sharp eye for detail is amazing and I owe you many many thanks for polishing my work!

Rebecca Van Kaam, what can I say? There is no one who breathes more life into my books than you. You motivate me all the time, to not just write for myself, but for others to enjoy around the world! You are a special soul and I thank you for all you do!

And as always, I thank God and my family for being with me everyday. I would be lost without you!

J. P.

Preface

The water was ice cold when my back shattered the surface like broken glass. The pain in my side burned as I kicked to the surface, spinning around, looking for the girl. I swam, turning and searching urgently under the dull light of the crescent moon. With each breath, I blinked away salty water and looked more, above and below. My eyes stung as I tried to focus, moving and reaching, but too much time was passing.

It had only taken a few minutes for the ship to be just a small light in the distance, and there I was, bobbing up and down, helplessly. The body of a stranger was lifeless and sinking somewhere close by. I slammed my fist into the surface and shouted in frustration.

A sharp pain stung with each breath, reminding me of my injury. I tried to focus on the unfamiliar pain to help me forget how I couldn't save her, and how there was a murderer getting away.

Knowing there was no way out for me, I let my numb, pained body, sink down into the dark water. The salty chill flooded my nose and then burned in my chest. I hoped this time might be when I'd end up at the bottom of the ocean. And for a split second, I thought I would.

Avery

Chapter 1

Even though my bed was full sized, it felt small, crammed in a niche and surrounded by walls on three sides. I tried to push away crazy thoughts of being in a box, floating on waves, and whatever else we were floating over somewhere off the coast of Cape Cod. Or the fact that there was no window for fresh air.

I hadn't planned on making this cruise, so I registered too late to pair with any of my friends, which was fine. But sleeping in a dark little closet somewhere out on the ocean was making me regret being alone. My heart beats were pushing my pulse between my temples and claustrophobia and nausea were both starting to kick in.

Just as I'd nearly lulled myself to sleep, my phone buzzed loudly across my mini nightstand, illuminating a blue light across my walls. As I slid my hand from beneath the down comforter, I exhaled a long breath, hoping it wasn't Leighton. But there he was, clear enough through my narrowed vision, caramel colored perfect face, short curls and all. Not to mention his deep brown eyes and signature smirk previewed right in front of a few simple words.

U up?

I pressed the lock button and set it back down on the built-in nightstand making a note to delete the contact photo in the morning. Maybe his number too. More motion rocked my bed. It was faint, but enough to cause me to quickly pull into a fetal position, hoping to not get sick. With the warmth of the down pulled high over my ears, I closed my eyes and began to hum, softly, a lullaby I couldn't remember the name of. The phone probably wouldn't buzz again. He'd be on to the next girl on his call list by now. Shaking my head, I continued to hum until it became peaceful, and then slowly drifted off to sleep. The next sound I heard was the escalating ringing of my 8 AM alarm. The only upside to making it to breakfast that early was that Leighton might not be there yet.

My cabin's tiny bathroom had just enough space to turn around in without touching the walls. After brushing my teeth, I glanced at myself in the mirror. Same dark hair and dark eyes, but it had been a while since I'd seen noticeable circles so dark under my eyes. Suddenly, wistful thoughts of being in my own bed, in my own home, popped up. But then I recalled hearing my sister's voice, just yesterday, playing up the trip. "I hear cruise food is to die for."

Jayla was so smart and mature. She took after my mother in every way. Down to her dark, straight hair and hazel eyes.

I had just sat down to breakfast and glanced at our mom's frown. "Well, I hope the food won't kill me," I had replied, trying to hide the nerves about the whole trip in general.

My mom then shook her head and pointed her fork at me. "No, it won't, but she is right that the food will be delicious *and* all you can eat. You guys are very lucky your school organized this for you. They certainly didn't have these kinds of trips when I was growing up."

Jayla swallowed a large bite of pancakes. "Yeah, you're lucky, so don't you guys mess it up. I want it to be available when I'm a senior."

I looked at her, seeing the disappointment on her face. She hardly got to go anywhere. Neither of us usually did. "Don't worry," I shrugged. "I'm sure you'll get to do something bigger. Maybe a trip to the Bahamas or somewhere. Not up the coast to Canada."

"You know," my mom cut in, with her elbows on the table and her hands crossed under her chin. "Cruises are wonderful vacations. There is so much to do on the ships that you don't need to go anywhere far. Besides, I'm less stressed knowing you're not going to some beach or island. Kids get into all kinds of trouble and dangerous situations on those trips. No, this cruise is perfect. Especially since I couldn't come along to chaperone." Her gaze shifted to Jayla with a wink, "This time."

My sister dropped her fork, letting it clink against her plate. "What does that mean?"

"It means by the time you're a senior, I'll be able to go. This time I have to stay behind, with you." She smiled.

Jayla hung her head. "How embarrassing. Just kill me now."

I laughed, but my mom's smile faded. "Jayla. Stop being dramatic and stop talking about death. It's the last thing I want to think about sending your sister on a trip without me. Got it?"

Jayla glanced at me quickly and looked back at her food. "Yeah, I got it." Dying wasn't something to joke with in our family.

My mom nodded and picked up her own fork again. She didn't say much else the whole rest of breakfast, and for the first time since agreeing to go on this trip, I had felt a strange feeling while sitting at that table.

It was a feeling that came back as I looked in the mirror, and I couldn't shake it. Something just felt suffocating and I needed some fresh air.

"Come on," I said to myself, swooping my curls up into a messy bun. I slid some flyaways behind my ears and rubbed the circles under my eyes. "Let's go do some living."

The ship was huge, but the hall outside my room was narrow and only lit by rows of dim, artificial lighting along the ceiling. My room was the last in a nook at the end of the hall. I pulled my door closed as my phone vibrated in my other hand. A chill crossed my hand and crept from my palm all the way up my arm, causing me to shiver and curse the cold basement they put me in.

The text was from my best friend Rebecca.

She was the epitome of a morning person. She woke up and went to bed with a smile. Usually thinking about her gave me a warm feeling, but the narrow hall grew noticeably colder. I thought about going back inside to get a sweatshirt, but hoped that once I went up to the top decks, it would feel better.

I slid my room card in my back pocket and tapped my reply quickly.

Another shiver passed over me as I hit SEND, this time causing the hairs on the back of my neck to raise. I turned around, feeling a tickle, unsure what to accuse other than empty space. An odd sense of cold gravity came over my body, and my mind began to feel lightheaded, tired and confused. I grabbed hold of the handrail, trying to make sense of the merging feelings.

I put my other hand on the wall to steady myself when the lights flickered. The cold chill came again, along with a swooping gush of air around my ears. It felt like the boat was tilting in slow motion, rising on one end of the hall. My feet pedaled backward, too quickly to stay balanced. My shoulder blades hit the wall just before the back of my head, and my whole body slid down to the floor like a quickly melting ice cube.

I sat against the wall, cringing from the pain between my ears and blinked away the dark clouds behind my eyes. My phone had flown somewhere, but I didn't bother to look for it. In the flickering lights, I caught a hazy glimpse of a dark figure. I pushed myself further against the wall as my mind began to settle. The lights flashed a few more times before coming back on to reveal a dark pile on the floor, just outside my doorway.

The heap rolled to the side, pulling long legs into a fetal position. Sounds of gagging came, followed by violent bursts of coughing.

Instinct prompted me to inch closer, still staying against the opposite wall. The person was soaking wet and shivering and the closer I got, the colder the air became, causing me to feel another bone deep shiver. "Are you okay?"

There was only more coughing and deep groaning. At a loss for words, I tried to get a better view and quickly saw his coloring looked all wrong. Super gray, deprived of oxygen in a bluish way that wasn't anywhere near normal.

I stood in the space beside him, trying to hold my balance against the wall. "I'll go get help," I stuttered.

Inching past, I was able to get a closer look at his face. He was clearly young, probably my age and in serious need of medical attention. "I'll be right back," I murmured.

As I crossed the space between him and the wall, he grabbed my ankle with a cold grip. "Please. Don't," he pleaded hoarsely. He was squeezing so hard that I felt the throbbing in my Achilles all the way to the pain behind my head.

A set of brown eyes darker than mine locked on my gaze. His face contorted in pain. One arm cradled his stomach and the other still gripped tightly around my ankle.

Standing there mute and trembling from either fear or the cold, I just looked at him. His hand was like ice, and still gripping my leg with a vengeance. "I'll be fine. Just give me a few minutes, please."

He was shivering now and his face was still contorted, but his coughing fit had stopped. He began to steady his breathing, his grip slowly loosening in increments, almost like he was testing my next move. Every instinct in my body told me to go get help, but I had no idea what it would be for.

"Are you sick?" I asked, staying completely still.

He shook his head just enough to communicate.

"Are you hurt?"

There was a long pause and then he closed his eyes, without answering. I bent down to get a closer assessment and he wreaked of salt.

"Is that ocean water?" I asked, and something in that question caused him to tense up and let go of my leg. "Hey." I nudged him gently. "You still with me?"

He didn't answer and although his color was starting to return, I had no idea what was going on, so I went to stand up again. In an instant, he grabbed my arm and pulled me back toward him. I squealed until he was eye to eye with me and in his eyes I saw fear, desperation and pain. It was terrifying. The same as when I had found my father and the memory flashed before my eyes and I fell to my knees. Tears and fear threatened to come out and I fought them both as I forced myself to blink and refocus.

The guy's grip must have taken all of his energy, because he collapsed his head onto the floor again and let me go. "Please don't," he sighed. "I'll be okay. I just need a quiet place for a few minutes. Please."

The words he spoke were a little calming, but many things went through my mind and they all led back to going to get someone, anyone to handle this besides me. But something in his voice pleaded with me and I couldn't stop myself from needing to listen this time. That maybe it wasn't happening to me all over again.

"Okay." I looked him over. "If you can sit in a chair and tell me what's wrong, then I'll believe you don't need help. Okay?"

He nodded and that felt like a good compromise. I tried to reach out my arms far from my dry body and lift. He flinched at my efforts, but slowly sat up with the help. I moved behind his back and saw my phone underneath him. I picked it up and slid it quickly into my back pocket, feeling the surface soaking into my jeans. I only hoped it wasn't ruined.

It took some more effort to help him up, but he did it and even hunched over, he was a little taller than me. Suddenly, I felt vulnerable. Apprehension hit me at the thought of letting this stranger into my cabin. I even visualized letting him go, but a little test assured me that he would fall completely over without help.

Danger comes in all forms, but instead of just leaving him there, I found myself whispering, "This is nuts." All while trying to keep him up and take out my room key. I swiped the card and pushed the door open from behind him. As soon as he was in the doorway, I steered him toward the leather desk chair. He plopped down and hunched over the desk like he was the average student, sleeping in class. Only it looked all wrong. Wet and wrong.

I stood between him and the door, watching, still feeling unsure. "Listen, I can go get you some help now?"

He put his hand up, showing me his pointer finger. I gave him several seconds and there was nothing more. Just him hunched over the desk.

"Look, just tell me what's wrong? Or I'm going to get a teacher."

I rolled my eyes as soon as the words left my mouth, sending a pain through my brain, but I ignored it.

"A teacher?" he asked softly turning toward me, his head tilted.

"Um, yeah," I blinked. "From the trip. School. I'm on a...nevermind. I'll get an adult."

Oh my goodness. Stop talking.

His eyebrow raised. "How old are you?"

I rolled my eyes again, embarrassed. It was a simple question, but it made me feel childish, and that was something I wanted this whole trip to change. It was time for me to be an adult. To take care of myself, on my own, without my mother worrying so much. I didn't want to tell him that I just turned eighteen, so I turned the question back to him, "How old are you?"

He looked at me, his dark, wet bangs sticking to his forehead. "Nevermind."

My weight shifted, feeling a little more in control of the situation. "Listen, just tell me what's the matter." He sat up a little more straight, put his elbows on the table and began rubbing one temple.

After several seconds of silence, he exhaled a long, deep breath. "I fell in the pool."

"In your clothes?"

"Yes. In my clothes."

"Why are you down here?"

He was still rubbing his temple. "I was looking for my room."

I thought about the tilting gust and lights flashing. Maybe I bumped my head a little too hard. He took a peek at me out of the corner of his eye and then I knew he was lying. "What's your room number? And why would you be coughing up water all the way down here? And why do you keep bracing your side?"

My phone buzzed in my pocket. I slid it out, thankful it still worked and wiped the remnants of water on my shirt. It was Rebecca, waiting for me. I texted her a quick reply and slid it back in my pocket and looked back to him for some answers.

"You talk a lot," he said, which was normally completely untrue. But he was right, and even though I was oddly curious, it didn't make sense for me to chase trouble.

"Look I gotta go meet my friend. Do you think you can get back to your own room okay?"

He took a deep breath. "I will be able to in a few minutes. Mind if I use your bathroom?"

I studied him for a moment and his gaze never wavered from me. He was there, soaking wet and in no position to do anything else. "Yeah, I guess."

He gave a half smile and pushed himself up from the chair with much better balance. In order for him to get to the small door, he pretty much had to walk straight toward me, so I backed further into the tiny foyer and tripped over my own heel. His hand reached to steady me and I instinctively braced the back of my head to protect it from the door. My shoulder fit perfectly in the corner for support while he had one hand behind my hip. My gaze instantly went to his hand, not because it was wet and cold, but because it felt firm, yet gentle and warm all at the same time now. As soon as he realized he was touching me, he pulled his hand away.

"Are you okay?" he asked.

Hearing his voice in the small space and so close to me, echoed deeply off the walls like a fine tuned set of notes. I cleared my throat, trying to clear all sense of confusion. How did I get here? Five minutes ago, I was on my way to breakfast. "Yeah I'm fine. I just hit my head on the wall right when you showed up."

His eyes widened a little and then he stepped even closer. "Did you see anything?"

"No, why?"

"Let me see."

I backed further into the corner. "No, I'm fine, really."

Somehow he'd easily managed to flip the focus off of his own condition. And yet, he was still gripping his side and now that he was closer to me, I could see a tiny trickle of blood through his white shirt.

"You're bleeding," I reached out and lifted his shirt without thinking and there was an open cut that looked deep and fresh. He grabbed his shirt and pulled it back down.

"I'll be fine. Are *you* fine?"

"I said I was fine."

He stared at me with eyes so dark, I couldn't see his pupils. They pierced me to my core, but his lashes were long and full, making his eyes inviting despite their dark intensity. While I was wrestling with the conflicting signals they gave, the corner of his mouth turned up slightly.

"Okay. Good," he said. "Then, we're both fine."

He blinked and nodded once before turning toward the bathroom.

"What's your name?" I asked.

He turned, only half way, and studied me for a moment. "What's yours?"

"Your name is What's Yours? That's a fine name."

He smiled, and his dark eyes gazed passed me for a moment, and then after a short pause, he murmured, "I'll be quick and then I'll be on my way."

The door closed before I could open my mouth. Neither of us had a name, apparently. So I just stood there wondering how playing a guessing game with a stranger could make me feel so confused, frustrated and exposed all at once. With a slight hesitation, I rubbed the back of my sore head one more time and turned away from the closed door.

J. P.

Chapter 2

Regret hit me as soon as I shut the door, but her personal questions had caught me off guard.

Meeting new people wasn't anything special. Finding my way around a new ship wasn't either. Lies had become the norm, so what was it that made me want to teeter on the side of honesty? It wasn't like I hadn't seen a pretty face before. Heck, I even trusted one or two more than I should've. Still, something about this girl drew me in like a schoolboy. It was recklessness and had to stop now.

I peeled back my soaking wet coat and lay the heavy pile on the shower floor. Next, I lifted off my shirt, cringing at the sight of the slit in my side. It was an open gash about an inch wide, and it was deep. The water had slowed down its healing, so it looked fresh and still bled when I moved. I pressed a dry washcloth to it for a few minutes.

Images of that scumbag killing the girl were ingrained in my mind. On top of it, my boots were soaking wet and had finally started bothering me enough to come off. I wanted to strip down completely, but would have had no clothes left. For the first time in a while, I felt vulnerable.

Just as I was thinking about what to do, I heard a door click open and then swing closed. I leaned my ear against the door, completely silent. Being wet, I could explain. A stab wound in my side would be a little more complicated.

Avery

Chapter 3

When he had closed the bathroom door, a few things ran through my mind, but I forced them all out and just took a deep breath and went with my instincts. There was no need to make something out of nothing. I grabbed an extra blanket from an overhead bin and put it on the floor outside the bathroom door, and then I left. But not before making sure to grab my wallet, just in case.

By the time I'd made it to breakfast, nearly half my classmates were funneling into the restaurant. It was the non-morning people half, and they were in no rush. I texted Rebecca to see where she was and managed to bump shoulders with someone else texting with their head down. We said sorry at the same time.

I looked up to see my ex's friend, Troy. I nodded and veered toward the side, letting people pass me. "Hey, you seen Leigh?" he asked. My neck shifted back and tilted sideways."What? I was just asking."

I don't understand why people keep assuming there was still any connection between us. We dated for a short couple of weeks and then he tried to humiliate me. I chose to move on. And every chance someone gets, they put us in the same sentence.

I shook my head and looked away just in time to see my best friend walking up with her signature smile. When I first moved next door to her, it took a while to not find her upbeat personality annoying. Being happy was something I was jealous of at the time, but it didn't take long to see she was the kindest, happiest person and that was something we could all use.

She looped her elbow through mine and blew her strawberry blonde bangs out of her eyes. "Hey what took you so long?"

I gave her a quick shrug and she led me over to a table where our twin friends were sitting in front of half empty plates.

"Hey guys," I said, distracted by the view of two shades of blue meeting on the horizon. It went on forever and was mesmerizing.

My attention was quickly brought back by the eerie unison of both Jenna and McKenna's voices. "Hey. We were about to come look for you." They were copies down to the exact way their hair cooperated in their messy ponytails, but they usually didn't act anything alike, so it was odd to hear them in stereo. I blinked away the creepiness.

All three of them raised a brow and waited for an explanation. I cleared my throat and looked out the window. "The view is really nice," I replied.

"Okay. Go get your food," Rebecca interrupted. "I'll come for round two with you. This whole experience is going to be amazing."

"I hope so," I murmured, my gaze roaming back over to the floor length windows.

"Why wouldn't it be?" she asked, giving me a nudge.

"You know why," I answered quickly, but as I turned my gaze away from how far the blue stretched, thoughts of the stranger in my room returned.

"What's a little fun without a little school drama every now and then?" She emphasized the word drama as she nudged my ribs. I fell back a little.

Long, firm fingers wrapped around my waist, followed by the buttery voice that used to suck me in. "Whoa, I got you."

I cringed, using my elbows to wriggle free gently, turning my neck slowly toward the moment I knew was going to be unavoidable.

"Leighton." The throbbing in my head from earlier suddenly got worse.

"Yeah. I'm here. Always."

"Until you're somewhere else," I mumbled.

"What was that?" he asked, leaning in closer.

"Nevermind," I said slipping around while pulling Rebecca by the elbow.

"That was harsh," she said with a chuckle.

I pulled her along until we reached the plates. "He's just so irritating."

"Come on. Guys without moral compasses will *not* ruin our trip."

Of course she was right as usual, but the whole relationship was such a disappointment on so many levels. All I could do was stare down at my shiny white plate.

She gently bumped her hip against mine. "Look, I totally understand what you're going through, but let's just pretend he isn't here and have fun."

I juggled a scoop of eggs, almost dropping some on the counter, and we laughed. "I'd love to."

After a breakfast large enough for three strong men, I just wanted to go back to my room. Then again I didn't really want to go by myself and wasn't sure telling Rebecca there was a guy in my bathroom, was a good idea. She invited me out to the deck which bought me valuable time to think some more.

The chilly breeze was exhilarating and view was spell-binding. I held on to the rail and sucked in a cool, salty breath and let it take hold of every corner of my lungs.

Rebecca sucked in a long breath too. "It's amazing isn't it?"

I closed my eyes, fighting the slight fear of heights and sense of nausea returning. "Yes, it is."

She nudged me again. "It's kinda eerie too isn't it?"

I opened my eyes and gazed at the horizon. "It looks nice to me." The reflection of the morning sun across the dark teal ocean was beautiful. Turning to her, I saw one eyebrow raised, right along with her signature smirk. "Well," she lingered. "They say this area of the ocean is haunted."

"Come on."

"It is."

"Haunted by what?"

"What do you mean by what? Ghosts of course."

I smiled, fighting the urge to laugh, but found myself gazing back over the water. It looked calm, the small waves rippling across the water in a slow rhythm that almost sounded as if they were singing a soft tune. A faint tingle worked its way up my back, thinking of how deep it went, and then I wondered what was really out there? "I mean what ghosts are you talking about? Just random ghosts?"

I studied the ocean surface, looking for any sign of apparitions or steamy beings seeping up from the water.

"No, not random. These are the waters near where the Titantic went down, remember? It's creepy."

Rebecca was a history buff. She could tell you about almost any event in history and make it fun to listen to. She was also a heavy reader of fiction. I will never forget the time she had me and a few of our friends over for a sleepover and told us a story about teenagers in a cabin with a serial killer on the loose. She kept talking about them until it felt so real. Every single noise freaked us out and we even started to think her father was a stalker. We slept with the door locked all night to keep him out. Just in case.

I had pretended to only be as frightened as everyone else that night, but the whole experience was terrifying and brought up way too many memories. The only positive thing to come out of having to prevent a full on panic attack all night, was learning that stories are stories and that I'm stronger than I thought I was. That didn't mean I wanted to hear more scary stories.

I shook off the fear before it could begin, deciding I didn't want to know what she was thinking up this time. "Rebecca," I exhaled. "Please don't try to creep me out on this trip with one of your stories. Wait until we get off the ship okay?"

She smiled and shrugged. "Okay. But it's not a story. You can look it up." She looped her arm through mine and winked, pulled us both off the rail and then gave me a tug in her direction. I walked with her around the whole deck stopping a few times to talk to friends. The different cliques were all talking about going to the game room and then meeting at the pool after lunch.

A small headache was reforming, so I passed on the games, but the idea of taking in the view while sitting by the pool sounded good. The only problem was, I wanted to spend some time resting in my room first. Not to mention my bathing suit was in there.

I told Rebecca I was feeling a little queasy and wanted to go lay down. It wasn't a lie, because the walk around the deck had me feeling a little motion sickness. Plus my mind kept wandering. I wrestled with myself all the way down the hall, unable to ignore the fact that the boy might still be in my room. *What's the big deal? It's my room. He's just a guy. Maybe he won't be there. Then, maybe he's the killer Rebecca told us about from the cabin. Just stop.* I shook my head, imagining all the bad thoughts falling off right along with the headache. This was ridiculous. He was just a boy.

J. P.

Chapter 4

I felt bad taking a shirt from her room, but I needed something to wear until I could find other clothes. I would've kept my wet shirt on if I had to, but when I opened her closet, the flannel shirt was hanging right there. I guessed her boyfriend would be pissed, but I'd planned to give it back as soon as I got myself up and running. Plus something told me it might be fun to piss him off.

My pants and socks were still wet and that was ok. It would make my story to the service desk more believable. At least I wouldn't be as cold. With my wet shirt in a small laundry bag, I made my way to guest services. I realized I'd been on *The Pristine* several times before and getting around was easy.

I was prepared to tell my story about losing my card and looking for it in the surf pool, but the young woman recognized me. I quickly tried to recall the last name I used.

"Mr. Smith." She cocked her head to the side. Smith it is. "Don't tell me you've lost your card again." My eyes went a little wide while I tried to figure out when the last time I saw her was. She batted hers and smiled.

"I'm sorry," I shrugged. "What can I say?"

She tilted her head the other way, tossing her long red hair with a smile. A few giggling girls started to shuffle up behind me, and her smile disappeared. She cleared her throat and lowered her voice a couple of notches. "Just give me your info, and I'll get you set."

After an uncomfortable few minutes, I had my new keycard. Not knowing what room it belonged to was normal, but for some reason there was just an unsettling feeling, that I fought off.

"Could you tell me what my room number is?" My heart was beating faster than usual. My arrival on this ship had already started out all wrong and everything felt off. It was almost as if this was the first time I'd done this.

"Of course," she smiled, moving her hair behind an ear. I looked away while she scanned the computer screen. The group behind me was young, probably teenagers, laughing and taking selfies while they waited. They were completely oblivious to the fact I was in wet pants and boots. What's the caption going to be? "Locked ourselves out of our room. Or, Lost at sea." Something to make their lives sound fun and interesting. There were a lot of younger girls also walking around, and my mind drifted. A contrasting image of the terrified girl I'd seen last night crossed my mind, and again, I felt unsettled.

"Here you go." The woman slid a piece of paper across the desk with my room number on it and a smiley face.

Once I thanked her and squeezed through the group of still smiling girls, I made my way to one of the ship stores. I picked up some off brand gray sweatpants, an extra t-shirt, black mesh shorts, a toothbrush, and black hat that said New York on it. I'd look like a total tourist, but whatever.

I asked for two bags. One for my new stuff and one for the flannel shirt, so I could take it back to the girl. I headed to my room, tired, wet and hungry. When I got to the right floor, the hall was busier than normal with a bunch of guys, probably a few years younger than me. It was hard to tell. They could have been older, but they didn't act like it. I stopped at my cabin and heard music coming from inside. Two guys headed out with music still playing in the background. I quickly apologized for having the wrong room and pretended to re-read the room number on the piece of paper in my hand.

My hacking abilities guaranteed I had an active keycard at all times on multiple cruise lines, but it only went so far. And this time, my room was double booked. Another sign this journey wasn't going to go well.

I maneuvered aimlessly down the hall looking for somewhere close to change. After heading up a level, I caught sight of the girl from the morning making her way down. My first reaction was to look at my still wet pants and shoes, even though I'd passed dozens of people up until then, and didn't care.

Her brown eyes widened when she saw me and slowed her pace a little, but then her gaze traveled down my body and locked on my chest. When her eyes met mine again, they had formed the tightest line I'd seen in a very long time.

She came to a stop in front of me, all up in my personal space. "That's my shirt," she declared.

I looked down, suddenly remembering. "Yeah, I was going to return it as soon as I found a new one." I held up my shopping bag to show her. "You would have had it back before your boyfriend noticed."

"It's not my boyfriend's."

"Ok, your brother then. I'm sor — "

"I don't have a brother either. Just give me the shirt..... Please."

There was a sharpness in her tone, but then her eyes began to water behind quickly batting lashes. Her shift to desperation took me aback. I had no idea why I was so concerned, but for a small moment in time, it was like we were speaking some unspoken code. And when she looked around to see if anyone was watching, that's when I knew she was also hiding something. Maybe she had stolen it herself. There was definitely some misunderstanding happening. I doubted she was a thief of men's clothing, and despite what it looked like, I wasn't either.

"I'm sorry. I'll bring it back. You can relax."

"No, I want it now."

"You want it now?"

She stepped in closer, and quietly, but firmly demanded. "Yes, I want it now."

I looked at her, trying to see if she was serious and then she began rubbing her head. People were starting to move past us and we shifted to the side of the stairwell which seemed to make her more anxious.

"You want me to take it off, right now?" She closed her eyes and nodded. It was definitely not my day. "Fine."

I started to unbutton the shirt half way down my chest and she didn't stop me. She was really going to let me take it off. I couldn't help but chuckle at the absurdity when she suddenly started swaying and reaching for the wall.

"Hey, you okay?"

"Huh?" she blinked. "Yes, I mean, I think so. What are you doing?"

"I'm taking off your shirt. Like you asked."

"What?" She put her palms over her ears and began to buckle at the knees.

I reached for her, and the next thing I knew, she's mumbling about feeling sick with her cheek pressed into the crack of my open shirt.

Trying to think quickly, I began walking up a level. "You don't look so good. I'm going to get you help."

"No!" She death gripped the back of the shirt putting enough pressure to lean me backward. "I'm fine."

"You don't look fine."

"I'm fine. Just give me a minute." She let go, but started swaying again, so I instinctively grabbed her around the waist for more support. "I just want to go to my room," she mumbled, "with my shirt back."

That was the last thing she coherently said before blacking out.

Avery

Chapter 5

My head pounded as I pushed it further into the soft, fluffy pillow. After a minute, I peeled my eyes open, realizing I was back in my room, or a room. Jolting upright, the pain rushed between my temples.

"You're in your room." The voice wasn't my friend's voice or anyone else I recognized, but something about it felt familiar.

I reached for the back of my head. "Oww. What happened?"

"You have a nice sized knot back there."

The more the voice talked, the more in focus it became.

The guy. The stranger, the thief. And whatever else, was sitting in my desk chair. He had rolled it in the small space between the wall and my bed.

"You don't have to worry. I just brought you here because you asked me to."

I rubbed the back of my head, remembering the stairwell and then passing out. "Why didn't you get me help?"

He leaned back in the seat. "Because you told me not to."

"Right. I did? Yeah, I did."

"It's starting to feel like this morning all over again, but reversed. Isn't it? You really should get that looked at."

"What?"

"Your head."

I rubbed it again, and it hurt pretty bad. "I hit it when you showed up, remember?"

He paused a moment. "How did you do that?"

"Because something knocked me off my feet and into the wall, and now I know I wasn't imagining it." I peered at him through squinted eyes, waiting for a response.

"Like I said, you should get it looked at."

"I'll get this looked at when you get your bleeding side looked at."

He smirked and I turned away.

"That's a good one."

"I'm serious."

"Me too. Head injuries can be dangerous."

"I'm okay. I didn't hit it that hard."

"Losing consciousness says otherwise. I looked up your symptoms and you probably have a concussion."

I closed my eyes and pinched the bridge of my nose, trying to relax.

"You need to keep an eye on it. If you start feeling worse, you really should get it looked at."

I shook my head as gently as possible, refusing the thought of seeing a nurse and them calling my mother. "I'm good," I convinced him. "I was fine at breakfast. I don't know what happened. Wait a minute." I looked around, remembering the shirt. My gaze settled on him. He was now wearing a white tee shirt and sweatpants. Socks and no shoes.

"It's over there." He pointed to the small desktop.

"Thank you," I said to myself, resting my still throbbing head onto the pillow, eyes closed.

The wheels on the desk chair made a high pitched squeal that got super close. "What's the deal with that shirt anyway?" The proximity of his voice made me feel like curling up into a fetal position with the covers over my head.

"You stole it. That's the deal."

"I borrowed it." His voice was smooth, like gliding its way through a casual conversation, but I felt defensive.

"Right," I lingered. "Whatever helps you sleep at night." Words were the only things I could think of to make him scoot a little further away.

He paused, but only for a second or two. "Look. There are times when I need help sleeping at night and it's the truth that helps. So..."

"What are you talking about?"

"I'm just saying. I'm not lying. To you anyway."

I don't know what he was even trying to say, but he didn't leave a question hanging, so I stayed quiet. And he stayed quiet, and even though I had my eyes closed, it was obvious he was staring at me.

His gaze made me feel uncomfortable. Partly because I was still so irritated that he was piercing into my privacy, making me feel the most vulnerable I'd been in a long time, but also because I had no idea how bad I looked.

"You don't have to stay here," I said.

"I know."

"Then why are you still here?"

"I don't know," he answered and then paused a moment.

My chin turned upward, so I could eye him under slightly raised lids. Maybe I thought I'd catch a glimpse of him without him noticing, but it didn't work. He was leaning forward, his elbows on his knees, his gaze locked on me. "I guess you could say I'm homeless."

Neither one of us moved for several seconds. When he saw me thinking and considering his answer, he opened his hands, palms up and gave a small shrug.

There was a slight sadness to his eyes and tightness to his lips that gave way to zero sarcasm. Still, I waited. He gave me nothing more and after another moment of silence, he leaned back, rested his elbows on the armrests and shrugged again. This time exhaling. It wasn't a careless shrug, it was a what-now shrug. It was a shrug that said he was waiting, or needing me to say something.

We were on a ship, so homeless didn't really apply, but something about the look in his eyes gave hesitation, like he said too much and wished he hadn't, but didn't regret it either. It was knowing that feeling that made me relate.

Between my stomach being flipped upside down and this strange pull in my chest, I felt almost drugged. Drugged or hypnotized to tell the truth. To spill things I never would or could tell anyone. Maybe it was because he was a stranger on a boat who I was pretty sure I'd never see again. Whatever it was, I felt an urge to tell him things.

"It's my father's," I breathed, unable to keep eye contact. "Or it was." I found myself staring at that blank wall by my bedside, and again the silence was thick and suffocating. I crept a glance back in his direction and his dark brown eyes were locked right on mine again.

"I'm sorry," he said.

"For what? Why are you sorry now?" Was all I could say, when what I really wanted to say was thank you for not asking me a million questions about it.

He leaned forward easily. "Because it obviously means a lot to you. If I'd known, then I wouldn't have put it on."

Memories were swelling so much, but I pushed them back down and took slow, deep breaths.

J. P.

Chapter 6

It didn't take a genius to figure out why a shirt was so personal or why she would have it with her on a trip by herself. When I'd seen it hanging in the wardrobe, I worried for a minute, thinking she was traveling with her parent or something. There would be no way to explain being in her room. But when I looked around, it was the only item there besides her stuff and I assumed her boyfriend left it there. Maybe I had wanted to cause some trouble. Why had I done that? She'd helped me. Kept her word about not calling the crew or other questioning people, and I'd repaid her by subconsciously causing a wave between her and her boyfriend. And it turns out, I'd done worse. I'd dug up old wounds. The worse kind. All I could say was sorry. All I should have said. But, before I could stop myself, the words came out.

"J.P." She had looked away to stop herself from crying or either letting me see, but she'd turned back eyeing me. "That's my name."

My real name. It hadn't come out in years, and I had no idea why I let it now. Maybe I was tired. Just tired of the lies, the constant facade. Maybe I didn't care anymore. Or maybe I did. I'd almost forgotten what that felt like too, and then all of a sudden a weird wetness welled up in the corner of my own eyes. But getting emotional wasn't my thing. I bit down on my jaw and took a long breath through my nose.

Her voice softened even more than when she said her own confession. "Mine's Avery."

I looked at her and there was a soft smile to her lips, but it didn't touch her eyes yet. She was hesitant. Questioning. And then she shrugged. It was a what-now shrug and I understood it, because I had given it to her earlier. Maybe that's what drew me to her from the beginning. I'd lived in the what-next for so long, that the present became a foreign moment in time for me. She made me feel the what-now again, and it was alive and rumbling so strong that I didn't care at all about the what-next.

I shook my head. "I think I'm in trouble."

"You just said that out loud." She had rolled on her side and was resting her head comfortably on her inner elbow, her brown locks fanned out around the pillow in long wavy curls.

"I know," I said more to myself than her.

She watched me, more alert now. "Why? You're not like thirty are you?"

"Do I look thirty?"

"No."

"Good, I was beginning to worry."

She held back a smile. Maybe if I left now.

"How old?" she pressed.

I paused, looking at her. How perfect she looked without a drop of makeup. "My 20th birthday is next month."

"May what?"

"May 4th. When is yours?"

"Mine is April 9th. This trip is sort of my 18th birthday present." She spoke like we were having a normal conversation and I suppose to her, that's exactly what it was. Her eyelids became a little heavy again. Once they completely closed, she murmured, "Thanks for bringing me back to my room."

I wanted to reach for the comforter and cover her up, but I just sat there rubbing my palms on my thighs, watching her fade into a delicate sleep. The bridge of her nose curved softly between high cheek bones and full, heart shaped lips matched her heart shaped jaw line. The natural tan across her face and down her arms spoke every bit of paradise.

Giving in, I covered her gently with the blanket and then I turned away to regroup. Her cabin was small. The smallest on the ship. There was absolutely nothing for me to do when what I really needed to do was find a computer. I had yet to research the news from the other ship. Did anyone even know the girl was missing yet? I wanted to know but didn't want to leave Avery alone while she still had that bump on her head just so I could go find a computer station. I ignored thoughts that said I just didn't want to leave her at all and started thinking about something else.

She had a laptop sticking out of a backpack, along with the charger sticking out of the outlet on the desk backdrop. I wondered if she had a password set to it and that if I used it, would she mind? Or would she even know or care, but the longer I stared at the closed computer, the more it didn't feel right going through her things. Not after what happened with the shirt. She was no longer just a face on a ship that was passing through. And that made me want to do right by her. I'd stay another hour to make sure she was ok, and then I'd be on my way. It was the least I could do.

As soon as I reclined the chair and let my thoughts wander, I was hit with images of the drowning girl, who I now realized didn't look any older than Avery. I had just gotten to the ship and made my appearance on the deck. It was late, so I kicked up on a lounge chair that was tucked away in the shadows. The wall clock read 12:15. There were no stars in the sky, but the bright moon in the distance caught my attention. There was something spectacular about the view of a glassy ocean at night that never got old. It was a peaceful moment until a dark figure approached and leaned against the rail. Medium height and slender, it was large enough to be a man. He appeared to be minding his business until he turned his attention to his right. I followed his gaze to the smaller figure of a female approaching.

She was walking while looking at her phone. Not surprising, I thought. But what I found interesting was after reading something, she looked around in all directions, like she was looking for someone. For a minute, she picked up her stride, moving closer to the man.

It wasn't until she was about three paces away that she stopped and looked around again. The man stepped closer. Her foot pivoted to turn back, but he grabbed her elbow.

"Wait," he said in a low voice. It was barely audible, but it was sharp enough for me to hear over the sound of whooshing waves.

"I don't want to talk anymore," the girl said. She tried to sound assertive, but I could hear the lack of confidence.

"Then why did you come?" the man pressed on.

"Because, you tricked me." There was no hesitation in her reply, but her voice did quiver.

"Did I now?"

"Yes. Just please leave me alone. Or I'm going to tell someone."

"That is unlikely."

"I will. I'll tell Erick." She stood taller then.

"What's the little sissy going to do?" He stepped closer, pushing his chest out with his insult and that was my cue to leave.

Just as I was getting ready to stand, she said something about parents and jerked away. His fist reached out faster than a snake, yanking her back by the hair and covering her mouth. She froze, and in a split second, he punched her in the stomach and whispered something in her ear. I bolted toward them, just as he lifted her over the rail. The horror of a mixed squeal and shout disappeared along with her.

My stomach collided with the railing as I looked below. The sound of splashing waves and hissing mist overpowered my ears as I listened for anything to hit the water.

"You bastard," I yelled, grabbing him. His pale face and icy blue eyes, the size of quarters, contrasted his dark five o'clock beard. My hands squeezed his coat with a death grip, the only reaction I had time to give before shoving him and grabbing the top rail to go in after the girl. Before I climbed, he punched me in my side, with a sharp blow. With all the force I had, I shoved him to the deck and leaped over the side and into the water.

Just as I was shaking the memory, Avery's phone buzzed on the desk. She stirred, but didn't wake. Curiosity was pulling at me and I couldn't help but take a look. A blonde's picture with the name Rebecca was steady on the screen. I couldn't help but feel relieved that it was a girl, and when it buzzed again a few minutes later, the reaction was the same. As if someone was standing by to slap the back of my possessive thoughts, there was an aggressive knock at the door.

"Avery! Open up!"

That was enough to jolt her upright. "Rebecca?" she breathed, confused.

"Avery!" She banged again. "Are you in there?"

Something was definitely happening, and I was trapped in the middle, literally. Avery became more alert and like me, looked around to assess the situation. I'd never wanted to bring attention to myself, but in that moment I strongly wanted to see what she would do, having me in there with her friend at the door.

We both stood, chest to chest, my back against the desk. More banging. "Avery?"

"Yeah, hang on a sec." She slid past, and glanced back at me and her unmade bed.

"Open up!"

There was hardly a crack in the door before three girls busted through. "Thank God, the blonde said. "We've been trying to call yo-"

All three girls, two of which were twins, froze. "Who is this?" The blonde asked.

"He's my friend. What's up?"

"Your friend?" She looked at me from head to toe and back up to my eyes. "Hi," she said.

I nodded which she only caught half of before she turned abruptly back to Avery. "Have you seen Kate Thompson?"

Avery shrugged. "Kate Thompson? No. Why?"

"Nobody can find her," one of the twins said. They were huddled around Avery and I could tell she wanted some space. Feeling confined or queasy even. I wondered about her head.

"Well, I don't know, I'm sure she's fine."

"Our mom said they've been looking for her all morning."

"Yeah," Rebecca agreed. "They said she hasn't been seen since last night. She went for a walk."

"Ok. It's a big ship. She's probably with someone."

"No," Rebecca cut in. "They found her keycard on the deck by the upper railing. They're worried she fell over or something."

I'd taken a sip of a water bottle and those words almost made me spit it out. I turned fast enough to rekindle some pain in my side. "What does your friend look like?"

All of their heads turned my way. Avery's eyes narrowed. "Brown hair, kind of short, why?"

My shoulders sank.

"Do you know her?" Rebecca asked.

"No, I don't. But I'm sorry. I have to go."

All of the girls moved aside, except Avery. "Where are you going?"

"I don't really know."

And that was all it took for reality to strike back. What was I thinking? There was no possible way for me to have a simple life. I slid out the door and didn't look back.

Avery

Chapter 7

Rebecca grabbed my elbow and spun me around, giving me quite a head rush. "What was that about? Who was he? Where is he from? He's cute. Who is he? How did you meet him?" I lost count of the questions.

"Avery!"

"What?" I blinked.

McKenna jumped right into view. "What? OMG Avery, who was that? We know every boy in school and he is not one of them."

This was going to get crazy, having to answer to not one, but three eager friends. And there was simply no way around it. I'd have to explain something, but I tried to muster up the best explanation that would make sense and get them off my back. Who was he? Where was he from? I had no idea.

"Look, I don't know. I was feeling a little queasy and I almost threw up in the stairwell. He just brought me to my room." All three looked at me with blank stares. "I'm serious," I said. "I just met him. Right before you came."

Rebecca studied me under low lids, thinking. "He's cute...I feel like I've seen him before..what took you so long to open the door?" Her gaze traveled to my messy bed.

They held back smiles.

"Are you serious? Come on. I was feeling sick. He was just waiting to make sure I was alright."

A long pause. "If you say so," Jenna chirped.

"So what about Kate Thompson?"

"She's gone," McKenna said. "My mom said they've looked everywhere."

"They couldn't have looked everywhere yet," Rebecca said, "but it's not looking good. If they don't find her soon, they'll probably cut the trip short."

That didn't sound like such a bad idea at this point. It had only been a day and it felt like five.

"Come on," Jenna said. "My mom said we all have to meet in the conference room. She has to do a headcount."

They gave me a second to grab my phone and room key and pulled me along. My head still throbbed a little and my stomach felt light and fuzzy. The feelings were oddly conflicting, but somewhere in there, was a new feeling.

The conference room was packed with tables all full of the graduating class, twenty teachers and twenty parents. Dr. Abney was standing at the back platform holding a microphone. Even though we were supposed to be on vacation, she was still dressed in a pant suit and matching pumps. Our assistant principal was walking around quieting down those who looked disinterested so far.

"Hello, everyone," Dr. Abney began. "Thanks for coming in. We need to meet with everyone to share some news and to talk about the remaining time we'll have here. To start, it's been brought to our attention that one of you has not checked in with your chaperone today."

McKenna leaned in to my ear. "Or checked in with her roommate last night."

"I want to reiterate that you all have rules to follow. Including an 11:00 p.m. curfew and checking in with your chaperone every morning and evening. In addition, all code of behavior rules carry over here. This is a school sponsored event where all rules apply and disciplinary actions will be enforced when we return.

"In a few moments you will need to find your chaperone and check in. This matter is extremely important for your safety. You may continue to experience your trip as usual, but we will be asking you to closely follow the rules and encourage your classmates to do the same. It is important to listen to your chaperone's instructions about what to do next. Thank you all."

"Wow," Rebecca turned to face us. "This could be a real downer. Getting us all in trouble."

"Trouble?" I said leaning in. "A girl is missing."

"She's not missing," Jenna quipped. "She just went out. Probably to meet a boy or something."

"No," I shook my head. "Sounds pretty serious and Kate Thompson doesn't seem like that type."

"Like what type?" Rebecca asked.

"I don't know. The type to sneak out and meet a guy. It's clear she's not with someone from our school. So why would she do that? She's kinda, I don't know. Quiet."

"So," Rebecca leaned in with a brow raised. "She's kinda quiet, so not likely to be hanging out with a guy that she doesn't know?"

I shook my head. "Not that I would think."

Rebecca leaned in further. "So we wouldn't expect Kate Thompson to do that, but we would expect you?"

"What? No. I wouldn -. Wait a minute. I didn't disappear with some guy."

"Look, all I'm saying, is people meet people. Clearly." She smiled. "I think we should cut her some slack. She's probably out having fun. Who wants Mr. Wells as their chaperone anyway? I'd be dodging him too."

I had to admit, that was kind of funny. Mr. Wells was the ultimate downer. He taught AP Psychology and treated everyone like they were in grad school. A very boring one. And he played mind games. He could convince you that you did something wrong even when you didn't.

"Maybe, you're right." I said. But when Ms. Jane, came over, I found it harder to convince myself.

The concern was there and she listed every rule on her paper with a shaky pen. We had to answer a bunch of questions about when the last time was that we saw Kate and that if we saw her again to tell her she needed to check in with Mr. Wells immediately. She was also very firm about our curfew. No one was to leave their room past 11 p.m., and she encouraged us not to talk to strangers. She then joined the group of whispering chaperones. In unison, my friends turned to look at me.

After denying doing anything wrong again, they finally dropped the talk of finding J.P. in my room. At least while we ate lunch. Nothing seemed unusual in the café and people were back to acting as if nothing was off. Even my friends started talking about going poolside again and sipping smoothies, so we tried one more time to plan for bathing suits and an afternoon in the sun.

I convinced the girls to meet me there later and headed back to my room. My floor was desolate and the halls were confining, but the last hour had been full blast and the peace was nice. How I let them talk me into partying poolside was crazy, but I was determined to find fun on this cruise.

Life was, after all, just starting to settle in for me. Although I don't think we'll ever stop looking over our shoulders, my mom was ready to let me go off to college and for the first time, the idea of being on my own didn't scare me. The cruise was my first step into doing things in the, "real" world.

A small smile formed as I rounded the last turn to my room just thinking about the future and then I stopped short. J.P. was sitting on the floor, legs stretched out and crossed at the ankles. His arms were also crossed and his head was leaning against the wall. I moved slowly, feeling a thickness in the distance between us. A strange force filled the space, like a magnetic pull pushing me away and pulling me in at the same time.

I was a step or two from standing over him when I realized he was sleeping. His hair looked like he'd run his fingers through it a few times. It wasn't long enough to fall back into place, so it just stood up in whatever direction it was pushed. His lashes were long and thick enough to make any girl jealous and his angular cheeks were chiseled, and despite him being asleep, his jaw was tense, making him look unrelaxed.

He was ridiculously mysterious and was outside my room again. I could have stayed there all day trying to make sense of things, but the more I watched him, the more I knew it was silly to keep guessing.

"Hi," I said, "Sorry, if I startled you."

"No, it's okay." He stood up with a slow ease.

"What's up?"

"I just need my stuff," he said.

"Stuff?"

"My bag. My keycard. I left it earlier."

"Oh my gosh. Right. You did." I felt so stupid. I didn't even notice, but that meant he didn't have a way to eat or anything. "Sure, come in. I'm sorry. I didn't realize."

It took me three swipes to get the card to work correctly. "You're probably starving."
I hurried in awkwardly, but he slipped into the foyer with ease.

"Starving is a strong word."

I practically ransacked my room looking for his stuff. It was partly to hurry for him, but it was mostly nerves at having him in there again, and wanting to look busy.

He came further into my room. "Really, I'm not starving."

I turned around, blowing some messy flyaways out of my eyes. "You're not?"

"I'm not."

"Oh, okay. Good then."

He stepped closer to me, watching me, making me feel really hot. "I have to tell you something."

I spotted his bag on the desk chair, but he didn't seem too concerned about it. I wanted to sit, but the only open spot was my bed, which was a mess from earlier. I started fixing it as he just stood there in awkward silence. After a minute of him taking deep breaths, he asked me if I'd found my friend.

"My friend?"

"The girl. The one who was missing?"

I shook my head. "Not yet. Why?" He sucked in another deep breath and slipped past me finding a made spot on my bed, leaving me standing over him, waiting. "What's going on?"

He looked up at me and exhaled. "I think your friend is gone."

"She's not my friend. I mean I know her from school. Anyway, what do you mean gone?"

"Nevermind. Forget I said that. I thought she was important to you." He stood, making a straight path to his bag on the chair. "I should go."

"Wait a minute," I reached for his arm. "Tell me what you mean. Please."

"I can't."

"Yes you can. You started to."

"Look, I'm sorry, I can't. It's all wrong. Forget I said anything. Please." He turned toward the door and was going to leave.

"Wait a minute," I rushed past him, making him off balanced in the small space and blocked the door with my back. He was going to have to physically move me to leave.

We stood face to face for a long while. He ran his hand through his hair a few times, making it even more messy. He was, no doubt, ridiculously cute close up, but he honestly looked like a mess. An agitated mess, and an agitated stranger was starting to make me nervous.

His gaze darted from the wall next to me to my own surprised gaze. He studied me again and then shook his head. "Look, I'm really sorry for meeting you like this. I'm sorry for everything. Taking your dad's shirt, and for your friend, especially, your friend. But I have to go. You don't want anything to do with me. Trust me."

"Why not? How do you know Kate Thompson?" He shifted his weight uncomfortably. "Can you just tell me? Please?"

He pinched his nose and closed his eyes, making me even more curious as to what was going on. I'd known this person less than a day and it was like he had a lifetime of secrets. My phone buzzed in my pocket, but I ignored it. Then it buzzed a second time. "Gee whiz. What is it?" I groaned, looking at the screen. Rebecca.

"You should get that, or your friends will come knocking again." He had a small smile that came with a wave of charisma.

"You have a point." But, I stayed in front of the door and swiped the screen. "Hello? They did? Where? Wow... Cool.... Yeah. I guess you were right... Okay. Yeah, I'm changing now. Alright. Bye." I slid my phone back in my pocket. "Well, good news. They found Kate Thompson."

"They did? Where?"

"I don't know. Rebecca said she texted her friend this morning that she was fine and just hung out with a guy she met last night." His gaze went to the floor and he leaned his shoulder against the wall.

"That's not possible."

"Why isn't it?"

"It's just not." He glanced at the ceiling, shaking his head.

"Well I don't know. But it's good news for us. Our chaperones might relax a little bit now."

"Look, I have to go. Stay with your friends. Ok? And don't walk around the ship alone."

"O...kay. But why?"

"Just trust me. Stay in groups."

And with that, he reached for the handle, clearly but politely asking me to move, which I did.

J.P.

Chapter 8

They said they found the girl and maybe they had, but if so, that meant someone else was missing. I know ships like the back of my hand and couldn't believe I'd missed it was the same one. It had been so late last night, all I'd wanted was to rest for a while. The deck under the moon was a good idea, until I'd seen the fight. What came next happened so fast I didn't even know what hit me. And I certainly didn't expect to be right back on the same ship.

I had slid out of Avery's room in a hurry and walked straight to the upper deck and confirmed it was the same spot I'd been last night. The lounge chair in the shadows was still crooked, just like I'd left it. And if this was the same ship, there was a girl missing. Who was definitely pushed overboard by someone who terrified her.

The thought of it made me angry. Someone stabbed me in my side and tried to kill us both. No matter how much I'd sat deckside, watching the ocean, trying to take in the breeze and clear my thoughts, each corner of my mind was filled with memories bouncing around. The girl, the man, Avery. The girl, the man, Avery.

I'd used needing my card and bag as a reason to see her again. A replacement could have been obtained just as easily as the first. What I'd wanted was to see if she was alright. Whatever was happening on this ship, she was close to it and I didn't like that. One day, and a lifetime of memories was overshadowed by the girl, the man, and Avery.

When she let me back in her room, I'd felt her emotions. Concern, nerves, and a little fear. All feelings that made me regret seeing her again.

Leaving had been the right thing to do, but it didn't stop me from thinking about her, even still. After getting something to eat, I headed to the shop and charged some more clothes, some generic Ray Bans and replaced my plastic bag with a backpack. I walked around the decks telling myself I was looking for the man who tried to kill me, but my desire to do that went out the window when I saw her sitting by the pool with her friends.

Even from a distance, I could tell it was her. There she was with her hair up, sitting between the blonde and the twins. Standing over them was a bunch of boys, drinking smoothies in their board-shorts, shell necklaces(on a cruise), and backward hats. I laughed to myself, but couldn't help feeling some resentment too. They could do whatever they wanted without a worry in the world. And they were doing it so close to a half-naked Avery. Her black bikini top was like a sports bra, but her bottoms were a pale pink color. When she stood to grab her towel, one would have to look hard to tell if she had full coverage in the back or not. Which she did.

It didn't stop the tall one from breaking his neck to watch her. Relief couldn't come fast enough when she put her shorts on and wrapped her towel around her shoulders. It was pretty nice out and she looked completely dry, so she hadn't done it out of necessity. I turned and walked away, unable to keep from smiling.

Later that night, I'd learned the school was hosting a party and they all went to the club and danced. They seemed to be staying in groups and I hadn't seen the man who forced me overboard, so all seemed good to the point that boredom set in.

Finding the only quiet place was on the deck again, I went to another lounge chair in a different corner and slept under the moonlight. I woke up early enough to watch the sun come up and then went to the gym, worked off some stress and took a shower in the locker room. It was starting to feel normal again, so I repeated the same thing the next day. By then, I was completely restless. Normally, I'd people watch and find a group to fit in with and party. Some days I'd work the exchanges online. But this time, I didn't feel like doing any of that. I had checked the news a few times to see if anything surfaced and nothing. After dinner, I found myself walking by the pool again and saw the twins with the blonde drinking milkshakes, but no Avery. She wasn't in the café or anywhere on deck either.

If I hadn't been so keen to the fact that a psycho with a knife was walking around somewhere, I'd have forced myself to forget about her. And maybe if she'd taken my advice and stayed with her group, I wouldn't have found myself worried about her.

Avery

Chapter 9

I went looking for J.P. after dinner. I hadn't seen him since the day before and finding him was like a needle in a haystack. I only knew how to get around the deck and the main areas. I found myself in the gym, the spa, the store, and every place to get something to eat. He wasn't anywhere. The only other place I could think of was somewhere in one of the corridors. I started at the top level and worked my way down. The further down, the darker and more narrow the halls got. It was still near dinner time, so most of the areas were completely empty. I was one floor from mine, when I found him walking right toward me.

He came up on me quick and even passed me to see around one of the corners. It was just me and him. "What are you doing? You're not with a group."

"No, I'm not." He looked at the empty space around me again and raised his brows. "I was looking for you."

He opened his mouth and closed it again. How silly of me to make it so obvious. "Nevermind," I said, turning. My back felt like it was burning from his stare, so I didn't want him to watch me walk all the way down the hall. The elevator was right there, and thank goodness it opened right up. Once inside, I counted the seconds until I'd be one floor lower to hide in my room from embarrassment. When I rounded the corner to my room, he was casually leaning against the wall.

"The stairs are always faster," he said.

"What is it?"

"You came looking for me, so I figured you had something important to say."

"Right." I shook my head, debating on whether to even tell him anymore. I crossed my arms. "Nevermind."

"Hmm." He eased himself off the wall with a careless shrug that contradicted his close proximity and came face to face. "Must have been important."

"It was."

He watched me, head held high with a downward glance. "What was it?"

I watched for a minute, still annoyed that he had the upper hand, but what else was I going to do? He had information. "Well, I wanted to ask you about Kate Thompson."

His weight shifted noticeably. "Go on."

"Well she has been texting her friends."

"And?"

"But no one has seen her." He just looked at me with a blank stare. "I just think that's weird."

"No one has seen her?"

"No, no one. And nobody thinks it's strange. She's apparently hanging out with some guy she met. It's just not like her. She doesn't usually have a boyfriend. She barely talks to anyone. Except her friend Erick. And he told Rebecca he thinks something is wrong. That she wouldn't be gone that long."

"Did you say Erick?"

"Yeah, why?" He let his head fall backward and cupped my elbow steering me away from my room. "What? What's going on?"

"I can't explain it down here."

After a few flights of stairs and fifteen minutes later, we were standing on one of the top decks. It was still daylight but the temperature was starting to drop. He walked me over to a lounge chair in a corner.

"I was sitting here on Saturday night. I saw your friend meet a man right there." He pointed to the railing. "They argued. I heard her say something about telling Erick and her parents or something. And then he pushed her over."

He was standing there looking at me like he just told me about his day. "Are you serious?"

"I'm very serious. This is very serious."

"And what did you do?"

He took a few deep breaths, but he didn't waiver. "I ran over there. Confronted the guy and he stabbed me in my side right before I jumped over."

"You're serious?" He nodded. "And that's why you were soaking wet the other day?" He nodded again. "Well what happened to her?"

"I couldn't find her."

If I thought Kate Thompson was capable of carrying and using a knife, I may have suspected him of something sinister. But it didn't make sense.

I turned to him. "How did you get back on the ship?"

"I can't say how I got back on."

"You can't?"

"No."

"You do realize how crazy this sounds? What am I supposed to do?"

"For starters, you can stay in groups. Whoever did it, is still on this ship."

The realization shocked me. The only person to have claimed to have seen her Saturday night was him. And I'd found him wet and alone. I backed away slowly, "I have to go."

He didn't move as I turned and made my way down the hall. One glance back showed he was still in the same spot, watching me.

Rebecca's room was one floor above mine. This was not something I could figure out by myself. No matter how much independence I was seeking. There was just no way.

I knocked quickly and McKenna answered the door. "Avery, hey. What's up?"

"Can I talk to Rebecca?"

"Uh yeah sure." She opened the door revealing a messy room with clothes laid out on both beds. Their beds were against each side wall and although they were narrow beds, the room was a good bit more spacious to walk around than mine. "We're getting ready for the show tonight."

"That's cool." Rebecca came out of the bathroom with wet hair and sweatpants on.

"Hey, where did you go?"

"Can I talk to you for a second?"

Rebecca looked at McKenna and back to me. "Sure, let me get my keycard."

She slid on some flip flops and walked with me down the hall and to an open area by the elevator. A mix of passengers and students were walking past, paying us no mind as we found a seat on a bench against the wall. We both sat shoulder to shoulder.

"What's wrong?" she asked.

"Listen, remember the guy in my room?"

"Yes."

"His name is J.P. Anyway, he acted like he knew something about Kate Thompson, so when I started thinking it was strange that nobody's seen her, I went to find him.

She leaned in closer. "And?"

"And he took me to the top deck and told me he saw a man push her overboard."

"What?"

"Yes."

"He said that?"

"Yes."

"Why didn't he report it?"

"I have no idea. He claims he tried to stop the man, and went overboard to try to help her. Said it happened Saturday night. And I met him Sunday. Back on the ship, and he won't explain how he got back on. And why isn't anyone saying anything?"

"Wow." Rebecca leaned against the wall, looking at the ceiling. Then she looked back at me. "He said he jumped in the water?"

"Yes."

"What did you say his name was?"

"J.P."

She sat upright and looked my way. "Avery, that doesn't make sense."

"I know. That's why I'm telling you. I don't know what I should do."

"Do you want to report it?"

"I'm not sure. It just sounds crazy."

She thought for a few moments. "This may be crazier than you can imagine. I have to show you something. I have to go get it, and I don't want McKenna to say anything to Ms. Jane, so I'll bring it to your room after I get dressed for the show." I nodded. "You should get dressed too. You probably won't want to be alone after I show you."

She got up and walked away, leaving me there to wonder. I'd been there less than three minutes before Leighton came and sat down, shirtless.

"Hey, you cool?"

I glanced over at him, wondering how in the world I let myself be any kind of smitten with his lines.

"Cool?"

"Yeah, you aren't going to cuss me out or anything, right?"

This guy tried to embarrass me to literally everyone we knew on social media. I turned, losing patience. "Why would I do that?"

He just stared, mute.

"Well, why? Could it be that you asked me to trust you. And two weeks later, you were humping some chick. Oh and then you told everyone lies about me to save face.

You're a piece of work if you think I'm even interested in being your friend." His eyes were still frozen in place along with his mouth. And just over his shoulder I saw J.P. walking in from outside. He spotted me at the same time and, without hesitation, I stood up. "Please don't keep pretending. I don't want to be your friend or anything." And just as I'd said my peace, I walked in the opposite direction of both of them.

There was a burning hole in my back, so I glanced over my shoulder one more time to see the back of Leighton's head as he walked away and J.P. going out of his way to maneuver around people coming in my direction. As I turned my gaze forward, I saw Dr. Abney and a few teachers sitting at a high table and chairs. At a separate table was Mr. Wells reading a tablet.

I glanced back one more time, and J.P. was still coming my way. Panic set in a little and I found myself stopped at Mr. Wells' table.

"Avery," he said setting his tablet down flat. "Everything alright?"

He was Kate Thompson's chaperone, and it was about time someone spoke up for her. Plus I wasn't sure what I'd gotten myself into with J.P. To be honest, I was a little scared.

"Mr. Wells, have you heard from Kate?"

He shifted his body in my direction. "I have. Yes."

"Have you seen her?"

"No, I haven't. Have you?"

I shook my head and stood fidgeting, unsure if I should get involved.

"Avery if you know something, you need to speak up."

The words trapped themselves in my throat. My mom would be so upset knowing I was putting myself in the spotlight, but she would also want me to do the right thing. So I took a long, deep breath, and exhaled slowly.

"Someone told me that they saw her being pushed over the railing."

He uncrossed his legs and stood up before I could blink, and I instantly started regretting putting myself into the middle of this. But she was missing.

"What do you mean?"

I backed up and glanced around. J.P. had stopped and leaned against the wall, still watching me. I completely turned my back, finding more courage.

"I don't know. I just heard this."

"When? Avery, this is serious."

"Saturday night, but I just heard it today."

"From who?"

"I. I can't say."

"Yes, you can. It's very important."

I opened my mouth to speak, but the right words wouldn't come out. It just didn't seem believable and I didn't want to sound silly. "It's just people talking. I'm not sure, but maybe ask Erick? He may know something."

"Erick Grant?"

I nodded, hoping maybe Erick had information. J.P. said Kate mentioned him. Maybe he knew who she went to meet.

"O.K. He gently took my elbow. "Come on, we need to report this."

He steered me over to Dr. Abney and I repeated everything. Dr. Abney stood stunned, shaking her head. "Mr. Wells, you reach out to Kate again and give her thirty minutes to report to us *in person* or else I will report her missing. Understood?"

He nodded and took out his phone.

Dr. Abney touched my shoulder. "Thank you for sharing what you heard. We'll find her."

They turned away, huddling together around the table. Feeling my job was done, I turned back to find J.P. nowhere in sight. Maybe I should have mentioned him, but nothing was certain yet.

The walk back to my room seemed like it took forever. Once again, the lower halls were desolate and every ounce of me feared that I wouldn't be alone. With a deep breath and cautious stride, I rounded the last corridor to find it empty. I exhaled quickly and hurried to my door entering with relief.

I straightened out my covers and lay across the bed with my eyes closed to think.

J.P.

Chapter 10

That was it, I was out. I'd gone far beyond what I should have on this ship. I owed these people nothing. I'd be dead right now, if that was even possible. But no. I ended up right back on this death trap, met a girl and actually told her the truth. Most of it. And what did it get me? Three days of thinking about some girl. Three days of stress. Three days of thinking I could change things for myself.

Not only was I thinking about some chick, I was worried about some murderer harming her or worse. Like it was my place to worry. I'd seen the look in her eyes when I tried to tell her what I saw. She was afraid. Of me. That's what trust got me. And I knew better.

After she left, I'd stayed outside long enough to settle myself back in to my usual state of mind. Long enough to forget about her, but when I'd gone inside, it was like a never-ending bad dream. There she was. Of all the places on the whole ship, she was in the path between me and the closest place to eat.

My gaze easily honed in on her like a beacon. She was talking to a guy, clearly having a disagreement. It didn't bother me in the least. Whatever they were talking about was their business. I stayed in stride even as she stood and walked away. She wasn't going to have an impact on my choices anymore. She kept walking and I kept walking and then, I saw him.

I'd recognized his five o'clock shadow from sixty feet away. Sitting there, reading his iPad. I maneuvered around people to be sure not to lose sight of him, my heart beating a little faster with each step. I slowed, planning to get a real close look as I passed, and then she approached his table.

I stopped short and swallowed hard. There he was. What was she doing? I gritted my teeth until they hurt. It wasn't my place to get in the way. But still, she was talking to the son of a bitch and there was no way I was going to just leave her there. I found a place against the wall and watched the weasel sitting there casually and smug.

She did most of the talking and actually glanced my way as she was being steered away to three more people who huddled around as she spoke. There was only one thing she could be talking about and that was the dead girl and me. I shook my head in disbelief.

She had no idea what she was doing or how close to a dangerous web she just weaved for herself.

I tried. That's what I'd told myself before walking back outside, no longer with an appetite. She did, obviously, still have an effect on me. And that was my cue to get as far away from her as possible. I checked my watch and confirmed it was less than seven hours until midnight, which was when I could leave. It would be the only way to put these last three days behind me.

Avery

Chapter 11

Rebecca came down to see me while I was still laid across my bed, face down. I pulled myself together and opened the door.

"You look a mess," she said, sliding passed me.

"Thanks."

"I'm serious. You need some rest or something."

"Yeah, I know."

She sat on my bed and tapped her palm on the open space next to her. "And you probably aren't going to get it after I show you this."

She crossed her bare legs and pulled down her mini skirt. As soon as I sat next to her, she stood up.

"I actually need to walk around." I looked at her, waiting while she paced back and forth fanning herself. After a deep breath, she took out a book from her crossbody. "There's no easy way to say this, so I'm just going to say it." A few more paces. "So, here it goes. I thought I'd recognized the guy in your room, but I figured it was just a close resemblance. I mean there are a lot of tall, dark and handsomes right? So no big deal. But those eyes though. Man, they are like black diamonds. Sparkling and what not. You can't miss them. And the eyelashes. Who has those? Anyway, I figured it was my imagination, and that I was reaching. Plus I didn't want to scare you or freak you out with some story. But then you told me his name was J.P."

She paused right in front of me. "What's that stand for?"

I shrugged. "I don't know. I didn't ask."

"Right. So I went back and checked something on a longshot and here." She flipped open the book to a page and handed it to me.

On the left side was a black and white picture of a boy. My lips parted and I looked closer. It very much resembled J.P. "Okay, what is this?"

Rebecca sat down and folded the front cover over my hand. "Read it."

Untold Stories of the Lost Titanic Passengers.

"I don't get it."

She folded the book back to the spot my thumb was holding and pointed to the caption. "Read it."

Joseph Percy Carter, 19, was last seen on the day of the sinking wearing trousers and a top coat. His mother, father, and sister perished in the sinking. Their bodies were recovered by the CS Mckay-Bennett and later buried in Halifax.

I read it a few times. "Joseph Percy Carter."

"J.P." Rebecca said.

I looked at her. "I don't understand. Why do you have this?"

"I brought a couple of books like this because I thought it would be fun to read about while near the waters. Remember the stories I told you about?"

I shook my head. "So you're trying to say J.P. is a ghost?"

"No, I don't think so. I mean, I don't really know. But he looked pretty real to me. You touched him right?"

The question made me blush. "Yeah, a little."

"Right, so he isn't an apparition. I honestly have no idea. I just thought you'd want to see this."

I looked back at the page. The image stared right back at me. A professional portrait with a clear display of his cheeks, his nose, and those dark eyes that even in a black and white photo, still managed to have a mirror shine to them. It definitely looked like him. But it couldn't be.

"Maybe he's related," I said, staring at the picture.

She stood up. "Maybe. But where's the fun in that?"

And there it was. Rebecca and her fun. A new mystery to solve, a story to tell. But it didn't feel very fun to me. I closed the book and offered it to her, ready to forget about him and her crazy mystery.

"You keep it," she said. "The story is interesting."

She walked to the door, completely uninterested in taking it back. "You coming to the show?"

I thought about the alternative of staying in my room, catching up on sleep, but I really didn't want to be alone. "Yeah, sure, I'll be there."

She smiled and slid out of my door, leaving me to stare at the book in my lap.

My fingers tapped the cover, adamantly not wanting to get sucked in to more questions. I laid back on the bed and set the book next to the pillow. Closing my eyes, I tried to clear my thoughts, first laying on my right side, then left side for several moments and then back to my right side. Eventually, I found myself opening the book. Staring back at me was a complete replica of the guy I'd let into my room earlier and who stole my dad's shirt. The resemblance was uncanny. I'd seen old pictures that resembled celebrities and they were pretty entertaining. Maybe this was one of those doubles and that was a pretty interesting thought.

Turns out this Joseph Percy Carter person had been traveling back to the states with his family. His dad was a big time banker and they had traveled first class. It said he had written to his fiancé in New York, two days before the sinking, telling her all was going well and that he was looking forward to their marriage the following spring. I looked away and took a deep breath and then kept reading.

At the time the iceburg hit, he was reported to be with his parents in their stateroom, but a fellow first class passenger reported Joseph's sixteen-year-old sister had been elsewhere and that no one knew where she was.

His mother and father had accepted life jackets, but both had refused to enter the lifeboats until his sister was found. It was later reported that his parents were on deck when the last boats were being dispatched, but his mother continued to refuse to leave.

An additional passenger claims to have seen Joseph walking around the third class accommodations without a life-vest. Following the sinking, his mother, father and sister's bodies were found tied together at their life vests with shoelaces.

The search continued for many weeks for the body of Joseph, due largely in part to a massive claim over his inheritance. Joseph Percy Carter's body was never recovered.

"How awful," I murmured, closing the book. Those poor families. Why on earth would Rebecca find things like this entertaining?

I sat the book down trying not to think about those poor passengers while I got dressed. I absently threw on some leggings, a tank top and random off the shoulder sweater with flip flops. The live show would be followed by hanging out in the pool area with free smoothies and water games. And somehow I was supposed to enjoy it after reading about the tragedies in that book.

Rebecca saved me a spot in the back row. She was with two other friends of hers. I sat down and waved. "Where are the girls?"

Rebecca leaned in. "Ms. Jane has them on a short string. Something's going on. McKenna couldn't talk much, but she's going to text as soon as she gets information from Jenna."

Jenna had drawn the short straw and had to room with her mom, the chaperone, but it meant she should have pretty good insight to what was going on. We sat back as the curtain slid open. Two women were sitting at a bar wearing flapper dresses and hats. Their curvy bottoms barely fit on the round stools and the boys were chuckling, no doubt entertained.

Before we had time to react, two young detectives dressed in trench coats, with perfect hair and smooth faces, burst on the stage to announce a murder in the club. A gentleman had just been stabbed in the cigar room nearby and no one was leaving until the case was solved.

All the patrons were frisked for weapons. One by one, knives and guns were being laid on the bar and confiscated. Women even had knives in their purses. Boys were watching attentively, and girls had their eyes on the detectives. My palms were getting sweaty, thinking about the real stab wound J.P. described. I tried to shake the thought, but those knives were put on display with no way to ignore them. The detectives held them up one by one, looking for blood before releasing them back to their owners. It would have been entertaining if I hadn't kept fixating on the shiny knife blades.

"I'm feeling tired," I whispered to Rebecca. "I'm going to turn in early."

"Really?"

"Yeah, I need some sleep. And I don't like murder mysteries."

"You sure?"

"Yeah, I'm sure."

I smiled and nudged her bicep before standing and sliding out of the back.

On my way down the elevator, I saw several teachers and parents huddled by the information desk, talking with security guards. I let my hair fall to my face, hoping not to be pulled over for more questioning. A prickling feeling went up my neck as I slipped into the elevator to find Erick Grant, standing right there. He looked up from his phone giving his long brown bangs a swoosh to the side, glanced at me for a quick moment and then went back to texting. I'd seen him around school in a couple of advanced classes, but we weren't in the same friend circle, so it was awkward on the elevator.

The button on the wall showed he was getting off two floors above mine. That was the guys' floor, so he must have decided to skip the show too. We stood completely silent as the doors closed and I pressed the button to my floor. I thought about Kate and the teachers gathered together with security. The need to know something was making me anxious. I cleared the frog from my throat and glanced at him until he finished a text.

"Hey Erick, have you seen Kate?" He paused and turned my way slowly, studying me. "It's me, Avery, from

Government."

"Uh, yeah, I know. Um no, I haven't. But she's texting me now."

"Really?" That sounded hopeful again, even though he said it more like a question. I smiled, but he just looked back to his phone.

"Yeah."

"Well, I know someone who said they saw her."

He looked up quickly and turned completely my way, putting his phone in his pocket. Another sweep of his bangs revealed eyebrows more shaped and arched than mine. I'd never noticed how perfect his features were either. Always dressed well, but never up close enough to see how put together he was. Even with the tired circles under his eyes.

"When was that?"

"Saturday night."

"Yeah me too." He breathed out a long breath and faced the doors again. "She keeps saying she's going through something and needs space. It doesn't make sense though."

"But she's texting you right? That's a good sign."

"If you say so."

"Well, I hope so."

"Yeah me too. I'll find out. She said she'd come by to talk tonight."

Word had it that she'd been saying that to people all week. "What if it's not her?"

He shook his head. "I thought that too, but she knows things no one else does."

"Are you sure?"

He started reading closely on his phone again, seeming to lose all interest in me. I went to speak again, but the elevator dinged and the doors slid open. He glanced at me one more time and stepped out. "See you later."

"Yeah. See you," I said between the tiny crack before the doors closed.

I had a feeling he was being pulled into the mystery like me, but I barely knew him. He'd think I was a crazy person if I ran after him and asked more questions. But I made a mental note to find him tomorrow and ask him what he found out.

My floor was empty as usual and my room felt even emptier if that's possible. It definitely wasn't homey, but it did have peace and quiet. I changed out of my clothes into sweatpants and a t-shirt, and put my hair back in a messy bun.

The odd exchange in the elevator stayed with me for a while. I laid down and closed my eyes and the images I saw there were repeats of Sunday morning and earlier this afternoon. The memories played over and over and over, bouncing all around the inside of my head, making it impossible to rest. I sat up and grabbed the book, flipping through the pages to the picture.

It was obviously not J.P. He wasn't a ghost. He was definitely a real person with weight when I helped him to my room. And when he practically carried me later, I remembered feeling his heart beat when my face was buried against my dad's shirt. And he bled, so he was a real live person. For sure, not a ghost.

I grinded my teeth in Rebecca's name for sending me on this wild story chase about who he was at all. And did I really care? The fact that I was still thinking about it meant yes. I shook my head.

With a big sigh, I grabbed my computer and started searching his name. Sure enough there were multiple Titanic webpages with passenger manifests and Joseph Percy Carter appeared on all of them as deceased along with his family. So no doubt, the book was non-fiction, but what did that mean for me?

There were two things I could do, and that was either forget about him and Kate Thompson. Go back inside my little bubble. Simply wait out the rest of this awful trip and hide behind walls that my mom taught me very well to build for the purpose of surviving. But surviving didn't always mean living. So what was more important? Surviving or living? I knew my mom's answer, but there was curiosity, fully alive, inside of me that had the fatigued nerves in my body coming back to life. It was more than curiosity, it was a rush I don't think I'd ever felt in my whole life.

It was almost like a moment that gave me instant purpose. Things weren't adding up on this ship. How could any of us go on as usual? I felt like real answers that led to real resolutions were the only way. Living a life where I could be free to be myself was what I asked for. At the end of the day, hiding behind walls in a tiny room at the bottom of the ship wasn't going to make me feel good about who I was.

J. P.

Chapter 12

It was half past nine when I finished eating the only meal I'd had all day. Now I was doing my usual of sitting under the moon on a lounge chair. It was the same exact chair I'd sat in Saturday night. Aside from a few couples strolling past, it was the most desolate place on the whole ship. Far away from the activities, food or drink. It was perfect for getting on by myself.

There had been a lot of times that were really miserable for me. Growing up, I'd had everything a child could ask for. We traveled the world living in luxury. Everything about life was perfect until I realized life is not an experience you want forever. I'd learned real quick that when it's time to go on to heaven, you shouldn't be afraid, because the alternative is truly misery.

The fact that a girl died shouldn't bother me that much. But it was the way she died that I couldn't get out of my head. Her murder rewound and played multiple times as I stared at the very spot she went over.

I could still see the image until a shadow walked into my view, stopped and turned my way. A book was tucked against her chest behind two crossed arms. I slid my feet off the lounge and onto the floor. She walked closer to me, standing within a foot or two, and I was struck still.

There was silence for a few minutes and then she asked a real simple question.

"What are you doing?"

I stared up at her for a moment.

"What is your name?" she pressed, through my silence. I cleared my throat, stunned that she was out here. "Just tell me. Please. Your name?"

"Um. I told you. J.P."

"What does the J.P. stand for?"

I looked around to see if she had anyone with her. It seemed empty and quiet. Still, she had me off guard.

"Look, I don't know what this is, but we don't really need to be on those terms. So..."

"What terms?"

"Personal terms."

"Your name is personal?"

Wow. "Yes. Personal."

"Really? Your name?"

"Look, I don't know you or why you're coming at me like this. So I think you should go back to your friends. Alright?"

"And forget about how you told me you saw a murder?"

"Yes, that's exactly what you should do."

She watched me for a moment, her gaze invading my personal space, tracking my face, my clothes, my shoes, my everything.

"Okay then," she said backing up.

I exhaled a small sense of relief that she would leave me alone. She shrugged, pivoted on her heels to face the water and kept walking. The closer she got to the rail, the more space I had to put my backpack on and find another corner.

"Fine, then. If you don't want to tell me your name, then maybe I'll jump."

What? I shook my head, ignoring her.

"Yeah, I mean then at the very least you can show me how you tried to save Kate and how we can get back on board. That's what you said isn't it?" She put a foot up on the rail, launching me from my seat.

"I think you are still feeling the effects of bumping your head."

"My head is fine."

"Then you're being insane."

"What's. Your. Name?" she said, looking over her shoulder. With one motion, she went to hoist herself onto the first railing. I grabbed her waist and pulled her back.

"This is not funny."

She was literally trembling against my side. All of that terrifying herself, just to threaten me for my name was crazy. Her curls blew against my neck in the wind, leaving me acutely aware of her physical presence in my arms and the insanity in my mind.

"What's going on here?"

"Mr. Wells!" she gasped, looking over my shoulder. I glanced briefly, cursed under my breath and then turned my back.

"Sorry, just fooling around," she gave a nervous laugh, but her trembling turned to complete stiffness.

I slowly released her and slid between her and the rail, putting most of myself between him and her. The same blue eyes stared at me the size of quarters while I waited to see what he would say. He stood mute, his gaze passing back and forth between me and her.

I took her hand, pushing her further away from the railing and him.

"Let's go Avery."

I wouldn't have been able to leave her up there with that scumbag, so when she didn't resist my lead, a huge sense of relief came over me.

"It's almost curfew," Scumbag yelled. "You need to be making your way back to your room Ms. Monroe."

"Okay, I will," she called.

With her book still in hand, she hurried up a little more in pace with me. I walked, with no destination. After several paces, I realized her hand was still in mine. A quick look at her was met with chocolate eyes boring a hole in me. I turned away and kept walking. She finally broke the silence.

"What was that about?"

"You tell me."

"What do you mean?"

"You're the one who almost jumped overboard."

"I wasn't going to jump."

I shook my head, walking between a crowded area of the deck. She gripped my hand tighter and pushed closer against me to fit between the traffic. "I wasn't."

"Then why do something so stupid?"

"I wanted to know your name."

I rolled my eyes, saying nothing, all the while thinking about how I could slip away from her. As soon as she was far away from Scumbag, I'd let her know how insane she was, and give her the send-off she and I both needed.

"Hello?" she said.

I kept walking. I felt her pull my arm all the way against her chest as she climbed on her tippy toes to get closer to my ear. "Is it Joseph Percy Carter?"

The shock lingered, making my vision see twice the amount of people around me. The noise of conversations were deafening. I shook off the confusion, let go of her hand, and kept walking.

"Never heard of him."

Her gaze was settled on me, her body shifted forward with pure interest. I could see her looking into each of my eyes and studying my face, and then her lips parted and she sucked in a breath. I turned to walk again, unable to find any words. I couldn't even come to think about what she said.

Within five paces, she had moved past me and stopped abruptly, chest to chest with me. "I'll jump again."

I moved her aside. "Go ahead."

"Are you serious?" she asked, launching herself back in front of me. Her brows were creased. I looked at the clock on the wall. A couple hours until midnight.

"Fine. You know what. You are right. This is insane. You are making me insane. And I don't even know you."

She exhaled, bringing a calmness over herself. I glanced down at her softened gaze. "I'm sorry. The truth is I don't want to complicate things. I don't want to even be on this ship and I really shouldn't be putting myself into the middle of some crazy mystery. I don't know how to explain. I guess I cared about something else other than just staying alive. And talking to you made me feel a rush of some sort. It was really stupid, and I'm sorry. Now, you can forget that this all ever happened." She nodded a few times, and then brushed past me the way we'd come.

I stood glued in shock, blinking several times. Who in the world was this person? I felt like someone swept my feet from under me, laying me flat on my back. I turned watching her maneuver through the dispersing crowd. She made her way to the door closest to the rooms. Someone held the door open as she slipped through without looking back. It was the most insane day I'd had as far back as I could think. Had I not been so frozen in thought, staring at where she'd gone, I would have missed seeing a very real scumbag slip through the door shortly after.

I rocked on my heels and looked up at the blessed moon, mumbling frustrations. The next thing was me walking through the same door and my hand stopping an elevator door from closing. I slid inside, met with the wide gaze of Mr. Wells and furrowed brow of Avery.

I turned, pressing the same floor as Avery's. The silence was deafening.

When it stopped on the main level, I moved to the side making way for Mr. Wells to step off at the only other lit floor on the dash.

It was either that floor or Avery's and it wasn't about to be Avery's. After a moment, he crept past me without looking back.

The doors closed, leaving just me and her. I was still too speechless to say anything coherent, so I just rode in silence with our gazes focusing on anything but each other.

After a long sigh, the door opened on her floor and I moved again to let her off. She stepped in front of me and turned around. "Why are you following me?" She pressed the hold button.

I shrugged, deciding on the truth. "Didn't want you on the elevator with Scumbag."

"Who? Mr. Wells?"

I nodded.

"Why?"

"You don't want to know."

She huffed and hung her head. "Right. You're right. I don't."

She released the hold button and went to turn, and I just couldn't stop myself. "He's the one I saw push Kate Thompson. Now you know."

Her head turned so fast. "That's ridiculous."

"That's the truth."

"Jesus." She pulled my sleeve and guided me off the elevator before it closed. "Why are you messing with me?"

"It's the truth."

"Well your truths are confusing."

That was an understatement, and too quickly, I began wishing I'd stayed right where she left me. But this girl had me acting out of sorts.

"What did you mean by caring about something other than staying alive?"

She threw her hand up and let it fall. "I don't know."

"Yes you do."

She shook her head and with one, long blink. "I can't say."

"Now, *you* can't say?"

"No. I can't." She started walking toward her room, leaving me standing, questioning and wanting to get past some invisible barrier with her. I put my palms out, submitting to this moment. To this girl.

"Tell me what to do to make truths less confusing."

She stopped, looked at the book in her hand and then glanced over her shoulder. "It's past curfew. They'll be sweeping the halls in a minute. If you want to talk truth, we have to do it in my room."

And then she curled the book under one arm and left me standing there.

Avery

Chapter 13

The last half hour had happened so fast, I really had no time to process it. Maybe that's why I invited him to my room. I was exhausted and just didn't want to stand in the hall to talk or have to answer to Ms. Jane when she did room checks. By the time I'd entered my room, alone, a pinch of disappointment hit me, but I was long over the whole day.

I sat the book down on the little desk, clearly remembering me threatening to jump over the rail. I shook my head. What was I thinking? He'd been just sitting there looking so disinterested, and so I'd figured it was a way to get his attention. I cringed just thinking about the stupid idea.

I walked back toward the door to kick off my shoes and noticed a shadow disrupting the light coming from the gap at the bottom of the door. It was just there, waiting. Ms. Jane would have knocked by now, so I rubbed my palms on my sweats and moved my face near the peep hole. Just as my gaze met the glassy circle, he knocked, giving me a start. He was looking down and even through the distorted view of the peephole, I could see his hair was messy again.

I pulled the handle, staying behind the door, providing a clear path to my room without showing my face. When he entered, he didn't turn around until the door clicked closed.

His breathing was calm, but had an edge of irritability to it. Mine too. I walked closer to him until we were nearly touching. There was one thing to clear up above all else in my opinion, because I wasn't crazy or unstable.

"I wasn't going to jump."

His gaze looked away as if he didn't want to replay the visual. "You said that already."

"Well, I mean it. It was just a stupid idea to get your attention."

His gaze came back to mine easily, studying me. "It worked."

I half laughed. "Right."

"So, what is it that you want from me?" his gaze didn't waiver.

There was a plethora of places to begin. A possible dead girl. Miracle swim and reboarding. Accusing a teacher of murder. But I settled on the book first, picking it up and opening the page.

"I asked you your name, because my friend found this." I turned the page around.

"Your friend? Jesus."

"Yeah, what's wrong?"

"It isn't me."

"You didn't even look at it."

"It isn't me."

"How do you know what I'm even talking about if you don't look at it?"

"Because I've heard crazy stories and people looking to be part of some crazy notoriety with those books."

"Rebecca's not like that. She's just in to history. And she's my best friend. I trust her with things I haven't told anyone. She's a good person, just trying to help me."

"Help you what?"

"Help me make sense of you."

"And you want to do that because…"

"I don't know. Why did you come here?"

"I don't know."

"So there you have it. I don't know. I'm just trying to make sense of you, and why I even care. And I don't even know your name! Ugh."

I turned around plopping the book down and putting my palms on the little desk. He shifted beside me, picking up the book, holding it for several seconds.

"This guy is long gone," he murmured.

I glanced at him quickly as he set the book down, watching me. "What does that mean?"

He inhaled a slow, breath through gently parted lips, and then turned his attention to my phone which was sitting on the desk. He pressed the home button, displaying the time of 11:18.

"Okay. I will tell you what I might know about the book. I know the boy in the picture has a sad story."

"What happened to him?"

"Let's just say he had everything you could ask for.

Happy, wealthy, a great family. And one night, it all changed in a matter of hours."

His gaze went to the floor, but he stood still, and so close I could almost feel his chest rising and falling with each calm breath as I waited. "It was chaos," he continued. "Everyone running and searching for their loved ones. Including him. His sister had met a boy named James from 3rd class, and their parents were beside themselves when she talked about him. But he could see she liked him. And she was a very smart girl, who knew what she wanted, so he covered for her that night.

"Then the evacuation happened, and because he knew where she was, it was his responsibility to go get her." He paused taking in a deep breath. "So he searched and searched. He saw horrible things. People locked behind gates, screaming and crying out with children on their hips.

"When the crew finally cleared the stairwells, people trampled one another to get topside. He'd found his sister coming up. She hugged him so tightly. By the time they got to the top, there were only a few lifeboats left.

"Even after all of that, his sister refused to leave

that boy. She clung to him recklessly, even when he tried to force her in the life boat. She just clung to him. Eventually, she was going to get in, her mother right after, but they started lowering the ropes. Those bastards were so impatient. So impatient. Then James, launched himself at the crewman, forcing him to hold the line for her. And they shot him, without saying a word. Right there in front of dozens of shocked faces. Carolina let out a screeching cry that broke apart the sky that night.

"Their mother and father were horrified watching Carolina lay across the boy as he bled out. By then, there were no more boats. The only thing he could think of, was to use his laces to tie everyone together. It was then that he'd realized he'd given his life-vest to his sister and had nothing to link himself with. He promised to go find a vest and return. They'd stayed on the highest part of the ship to wait for him. That was the last time he saw them.

"When the ship broke apart, people were knocking each other with flailing fists and elbows. Others were pushing each other down like stepping stones looking for people with life vests. It didn't matter. Having a life vest was useless anyway. It was just too cold."

He blinked and the only thing I could do was stand completely still for fear he'd pull back. It felt like forever before he continued.

"A young mother was floating nearby, struggling to hold a small child above the freezing water. He was scared, but he swam toward them, noticing a porcelain tub barely staying afloat on its side. He grabbed the back of the woman's vest and pulled her toward the tub. He was so tired by then. So tired, and so cold he could barely feel his hands, but the child was crying and she was crying. He'd used everything he had to hoist them both into the tub, rocking it upright. Her eyes widened and her gaze tore into his. 'Thank you,' she cried. He'd closed his eyes, exhausted, but she grabbed his icy collar and shouted, 'Look at me Sir! Look at me!' The echoes carried as she kept repeating.

"He finally opened his eyes and was met with the darkness of hers only a few inches away. 'You will not perish,' she said. 'You will forever live above this water. *Never* to perish.' With those words, he closed his eyes and gave the rocking tub a push away from the chaos."

He let out a long sigh and looked back at me with a tight jaw. "And that boy is gone now."

He swallowed and I blinked a dozen times, looking around and back toward him again, swallowing once more. He told the story pretty quickly, like it would pass over, but it wasn't going to. I was far too drawn in. "Is that boy standing here, right now?"

He shook his head. "J.P. is standing here now."

"But it was Joseph Percy Carter, who you were talking about?" He nodded, checking the time on the phone again. "Let me ask you this. Could Joseph Percy Carter have lived that night?"

He looked at me one more time. "I have to go," and he slipped around me toward the door. I beat him there, blocking his path again.

"You can't just tell me something like that and leave. And I have more questions. Mr. Wells? Kate Thompson. You can't leave."

He went to move again and was stopped still by a knock at the door. "Avery, room check. You in there?"

"It's Ms. Jane," I whispered. I turned to the door, opening it with a crack, "Yes, I'm in."

She was wearing pajamas. "Okay, night."

"Night."

I closed the door and turned back around, "Please don't go yet."

He didn't say anything else, and he didn't move either.

And there it was again, the voice in my head, talking to me, urging, "Please."

He watched me for a long while, and then pointed his thumb toward the bathroom. "Do you mind if I?"

"Of course not."

"I'm going to regret this," he said, not moving.

I smiled, reaching past him and pushing open the narrow door.

He was only in there for a minute or so, when there was another knock at the door. I looked through the peep hole to see and sucked in a short breath.

Mr. Mathews, my English teacher, and Mr. Wells were standing side by side in regular clothes.

I opened the door a couple of inches with brows raised, gaze passing back and forth between the two.

Mr. Wells cleared his throat. "Avery, we have to do manual room checks. With every student. Kate Thompson was officially declared missing this evening."

"Oh my gosh."

I looked down at the floor. Hearing it out loud, confirmed what I'd already feared and made it feel that much closer.

"Yes, all students need to remain in their rooms and security would like to speak to anyone who last saw her tomorrow."

He looked at me, waiting. I shrugged. "I haven't seen her. Not since school."

"But you know something about her last whereabouts?"

"Only what I already told you. I just heard talk. I told you everything I know."

Mr. Wells stepped forward. "Yes. Right. And they're looking for the man you say she may have met. What about your friend?"

"My friend?"

"The young man you were just with on the deck."

"What about him?"

"Someone described maybe seeing her with him."

"Described? How?"

"Just a similar description of what he looked like."

"He shares a similar description of a lot of people."

Mr. Wells' eyes narrowed, and he looked over my head. "It wasn't anyone from our school. So we may want to consider why this person would also talk to other students."

"You know. Now that you mention it. That guy you're talking about has a twin brother." His gaze darted back to mine, a little more brightly.

"Really?"

"Yes, and he hasn't seen him since Saturday either. So we started talking about the coincidence. My friend missing. His brother missing. That's how I know him."

"He has a twin?"

Mr. Mathews spoke for the first time. "If there is a second person missing, we should report it."

"He already has."

Mr. Wells turned his neck super fast to look at me. "He did, but he's not worried. He says the worst that could have happened was that he fell overboard, but he's a competitive swimmer, and his phone is waterproof so he'd call for help if that were the case. So he's probably fine. Unless something else happened to him?"

I raised my brow and settled a long gaze on Mr. Wells, studying him. He stepped backward. "Thank you Avery. You will need to report for breakfast to check in. And they've ordered every passenger to remain on the ship even when we dock at the upcoming stops. Be sure to keep near Ms. Jane."

I nodded, "Got it. Thanks."

I felt like sliding my back down the door once it shut. I closed my eyes completely rattled.

"So it was my twin who got stabbed and jumped in the water?" I opened my eyes to see the cocked head of J.P., and him smirking at me.

I nodded, "Yes, your twin. Joseph Percy Carter."

He laughed. "That was clever."

I sighed, watching him. Intrigue was coming off of him in waves. "Ok then. You told me how the boy in the picture died. Now how about you tell me about J.P.?"

He bit his lip, considering, and then he casually walked over to the desk, checked the time on the phone again, and said. "I might as well."

It was 12:01a.m.

J. P.

Chapter 14

She had covered for me with Scumbag for no reason. I'd never had anyone do that for me, and I liked it. I liked her. And I knew it was all wrong, but I liked her anyway.

She was different from anyone I'd met. Much more intuitive than a usual eighteen year old. She stumped me. Confused and challenged me. And maybe that's what sucked me in. It was too late for me to go anywhere, so I sat down on the edge of her bed, giving in to whatever it was.

When she sat beside me, it felt like a warm fire next to me. I swallowed, unsure how the rest of the truth would go for her, or me.

"Tell me about you," she said.

It was a simple question for most, but I found the words stuck. "It's complicated," I said.

"Try me," she breathed.

That's when I realized something. And it was true. "J.P. was born Sunday," I said, "When he met you."

Her gaze cut to me sharply.

"When I met you, something wanted me to tell you my real name. And that's the best I could come up with."

"So what *is* your real name?" She turned to me, her hair had mostly fallen loose. She was beautiful. I turned away, unable to stop.

"You already know."

She stood and paced the floor a few times, and then came out of her sweatshirt. "It's hot as hell in here," she murmured. A white tank was underneath, fitted, but loose enough not to feel inappropriate to look at her in. She paced a few more times and then wheeled the desk chair over to me and sat right in front of me.

"Okay. I'm trying very hard to believe what is really potentially the most outrageous story known to anyone sane. But, I see something in you that I recognize. I know what it's like to hide things from the past for so long you almost forget who you are." She looked down for a moment and took a deep breath. "And so, I'm just going to ask one more time. She looked straight at me. "Are you Joseph Percy Carter? Please don't run me in circles."

Her eyes were soft and watered over. This answer mattered to her. More than usual. I don't think she was searching for some crazy story to believe in or shout to whoever would listen. She wanted to connect with someone. To understand. She needed it. Like I needed it and never knew until then.

I felt the moisture in my eyes at the thought of doing something I'd never done, and then I nodded one time.

Her eyes widened, but she quickly relaxed with a breath. "But how?"

I shrugged.

"I mean how are you here, right now? Sitting here."

"It's what the woman said. Whatever she said to me worked. And I can't die and I can't leave the water."

She blinked. "What does that mean, exactly? Tell me the science version."

"When a ship docks, or I die, I just end up on some random ship in the vicinity of this area. And so on." I looked down. "And so on. Except this time, I ended up on the same ship again."

"So you died?" She looked at my side. "From the stab wound?"

"No, that hurt like a son of a gun. But the drowning killed me, eventually."

She covered her mouth with both hands. "That's horrible. Oh my God."

She had no idea that I'd gotten used to what it feels like to take your last breath and to blink for the last time, but the real horror was the coming back. She looked mortified, feeling far too sorry for me, so I stood up and lifted my shirt.

"It's not all bad."

Her finger tips went to the exact spot where the gash had been. "It's gone," more to herself than me.

I took her hand and placed it in her lap while sitting back down. "It heals quickly. Always."

She continued to shake her head in disbelief. "Have you told this to anyone before?"

I smiled easily. "Absolutely not."

She glanced over at the book again and back to me. "But what about your fiancé? What would she have done?"

That question, out of all the questions, threw me off the most, because I hadn't thought about her in years. Many, many, years. After the sinking, it took me a week to make sense of what was happening to me. How I couldn't get off a ship, how it all led back to the woman who cursed me. By the time I figured it out, I went to write her to tell her I was ok and to ask for help. But I'd read that she was engaged again to another son of a wealthy banker. After a week. And to top it off, they married six months later in some grand New York wedding. I'd convinced myself that she had needed to find someone else to marry to provide for her, but her family was as wealthy as mine, so there was zero excuse. And once I figured that out, I hadn't looked back. I sucked in a deep breath and exhaled the memory, hopefully for the last time.

Avery was watching me, waiting. I kept it simple. "So to answer your question, she moved on before I could write her."

"Moved on? Did she know you were alive?"

"Like I said. She moved on before I could write. Ring and all." I acted like it didn't bother me, but it had. I was hurt, confused, angry and lost for a long time.

Eventually, I realized she wasn't for me. Her husband went bankrupt and killed himself and she married someone else shortly after that.

Her brow was creased as she thought about my words and then she shook her head, refocusing.

"And you told no one else?"

"No."

"So no one knew you were still alive?"

"My uncle did. I wrote a letter to him after he received my entire inheritance and told him I was alive, but that I didn't want to come back to my old life. I told him to deposit thirty percent of my worth into an account for me, and that he could keep the rest as long as he told no one I was alive. If he didn't follow the exact instructions, I'd return and claim it all."

"And?"

"He didn't believe me at first, so I had a picture taken of me holding a current newspaper and sent it to him."

"And?"

"And he did what I asked."

"And that's it? He didn't try to find you?"

"Why would he? He became a very wealthy man."

"J.P. I don't even know what to say."

The fact that she called me J.P. was more than enough. I didn't want to be remembered as a guy in an old black and white photo. A poor guy who really lost everything in one night. The reality of it was that he was long gone. I was nowhere near the same person from back then. She saw me for who I was now.

Only someone living years in complete repetitive torture could understand. Even the smallest moments could make the biggest difference. And she was making the biggest difference and I gravitated to it like a moth to a flame. But then she positioned herself in front of my gaze.

"So, what happens when this ship docks?"

And there it was. The reality that was unavoidable. The reality that would make having told her the truth a complete waste of time, and a mistake. I went to stand, but she pressed on my thighs and held me still with her palms. "What happens?"

I looked at her, seeing her eagerness to know. It was a painful reality that I'd pushed down for many years, and it was all hitting me again, like a ton of bricks.

"You leave. And I stay," I said.

"That's it?"

"That's it."

"Do you time jump?"

I laughed, shaking my head. "No."

"I'm serious. So you are here or somewhere, in real time?"

"Yes."

"Then I can find you again."

Her naïve answer shocked me and I stood up too quickly for her to hold me down. She jumped up. "I can find you," she repeated.

"You don't know what you're saying."

"Yes, I do." She held my arms and positioned herself beneath my shifting gaze very much in my personal space again. "Look at me," she urged and then paused. "My name is Johanna Roberts." I processed her words, settling my gaze onto her.

"What are you talking about?"

"My name is Johanna. I was born in Austin, Texas. One day when I was ten, I stayed home sick. My mom was on a field trip with my sister and my dad had to work. He said he had to tie up some loose ends at the office and then was going to take me to the doctor. I went to work with him that morning and was laid up in the back office, watching T.V.

"The front bell rang shortly after that, and he told me to stay in the back while he met with some people. I heard a loud bang just minutes later. I didn't know at the time what it was, but it scared me, so I hid." Her eyes were watering, but she kept going, talking almost too fast for me to keep up.

"It turns out, he was unknowingly handling money for very crooked people. Drug dealers, law enforcement. You name it. I testified against the people who killed him, and we've been living under witness protection ever since. I've never told this to anyone. Not even Rebecca. All she knows is we ran from someone. She doesn't know my real name. Only you do and so help me God if you tell anyone, I could die. So I swear, if you're lying to me, and I can't trust you, then I may as well be dead. So, if you're telling me the truth, then I swear to find you again."

"Are you serious?"

"Yes, I'm serious." She had lost her usual confidence and was starting to breathe deeply.

"The flannel?"

"Yes, it was my dad's."

I instantly remembered the look on her face when she'd thought I'd stolen it.

I hung my head and then looked at her again.

She tilted toward me, and I pulled her closer to me, feeling her shaking. With my arms around her, she fell into my chest and grabbed my waist like she was hanging on to every memory she had. I could sense her fears, her sorrows, her frustrations. It was melting into me. None of my memories measured up to how she made me feel. I took my hand and cradled her hair.

After taking in feelings I didn't recognize, I asked her one question. "So what do you want me to call you?"

She laughed in my chest. "The person I am now is Avery, so..."

"Ok."

Avery

Chapter 15

There was an indescribable feeling of comfort. I wanted to wrap myself in him like he was a blanket in winter. Everything about him made me feel more alive, from my toes to the top of my hair. I found myself pulling his face into mine. I started with my lips pressed against his cheek and he moved his mouth over mine gently, but eagerly, and we stood at the foot

of my bed kissing like we'd done it a million times. The heat rose up my back until I couldn't stand the sweatpants any longer. They came off as fast as my socks.

In a bold motion that was foreign to me, I lifted his shirt over his head and fell on him as he let himself fall onto my bed. He kissed me like there was no tomorrow and whether or not there was, was of no importance to me. My walls came down as he cradled me close to the warmth of his chest.

Just that feeling alone was nothing like I'd ever experienced before and may not again. It was Joseph and Johanna meeting J.P. and Avery. It was the most perfect moment, with the most perfect stranger who was no longer a stranger to me. By the time we fell asleep, it felt like our souls had merged to one.

My preset alarm went off as usual, alerting me to a new reality. I pressed the off button on my phone and glanced at J.P. He was lying with most of his body out of the covers. He had one hand behind his head and he watched me under a low gaze that teetered between lazy and cautious.

We were silent for a long moment, me wondering what this new day would bring. I smoothed back some curls that brushed the side of my face. "This is awkward."

He pursed his lips in a ridiculously hot way that parked my gaze on them.

"Do you mean to tell me you don't make a habit of waking up next to hundred-year-old permanent sailors?"

I laughed, "No, I do not."

"Would you hand me my cane?"

"Stop," I was still laughing.

"I'm just saying."

"I think you'll get around just fine." I stood up, setting my phone back on the desk and gathered some clothes. I freshened up and took a short shower with a cheesy smile plastered on my face the entire time.

I dressed in dark washed shorts and a thin, pink cotton shirt layered over a white cami. I left my hair down to dry and went back into the room. J.P. was rolled on his side, sleeping like a rock. I imagined how tired he was. How exhausting being in his position would be.

The closet creaked on the rails as I slowly tried to slip my dirty clothes into my laundry bag. When I turned around, he was rolled onto his back, watching me.

He stood up and looped his hand through one of his backpack straps and walked toward me. He slid past me in the small space with a well formed smirk as he closed the bathroom door.

I was in so much trouble. The train was barreling down the tracks and I was holding on with my fingertips.

When I checked my phone, I had three missed texts and a missed call from Rebecca. I opened a reply and began typing, but was jolted by banging on my door.

"Avery!"

"Jeez." What is with these people and my room?

I checked the peep hole and Rebecca was there bouncing on her heels. As soon as I pulled the door open, she whizzed past with a gust of a sweet vanilla scent.

"What's up?"

"You are not going to believe this."

She had tears in her eyes. "What is it?"

"Erick Grant killed himself last night."

"He what?"

"Yes. His roommate found him this morning in the bathroom."

"That doesn't make sense. I just saw him yesterday in the elevator. He seemed fine. He actually said he was texting Kate Thompson."

Rebecca opened her mouth to respond, but then turned her ear toward the bathroom. "Is there someone in there?"

My gaze directed to a far corner in the ceiling.

"Avery?"

When I looked back to her, she was looking at my bed and I rolled my eyes. Her gaze then settled on the book on my desk.

"Is it him?"

I nodded

"Avery!" she half hissed. "Did you ask him about this?"

"I did."

"And?"

And, I stood mute, a little unprepared to answer.

"And? Tell me what he said."

I was still quiet when we heard the knob click on the bathroom door. We both turned to find J.P. standing there with wet hair and no shirt.

He gave Rebecca a nod and slipped by us to put on the t-shirt that was pooled on the floor. We both watched him closely, waiting to figure out what to say next. Rebecca cleared her throat.

"I can go, and let you guys finish up here."

He turned, fully dressed. "You don't have to leave." And then he turned to me. "I heard what you guys said." He sat on the bed, put on his shoes and then walked over to me. Rebecca pressed herself closer to the desk. "Do you trust her?" he asked.

I blinked and looked at her and then back to him. "Yes."

He swallowed and took a deep breath. "Then you

can tell her." He slid past me, putting on his backpack when he got to the door. "I have something to look in to. I'll find you later."

It felt like he may slip out and that I may not see him again and it worried me, so I followed after him as he opened the door. He stopped and I just wrapped my arms around his body. He froze a moment when my face touched his neck, but after a moment he put his arms around me pressing out the anxiety and then he left.

I turned back to see Rebecca standing with her bottom lip loosely hanging. "Oh.My.God. I leave you alone for a few hours."

"What did you expect?" I shrugged.

She shook her head and spun the desk chair around. "Sit."

And so I did, taking my time recounting every word in J.P.'s story. When I was done, she stood there with her arms crossed and eyes wide.

"I can't even believe this."

"I know."

"And you believe this?" she asked.

I shrugged. "He was remembering, Rebecca. And he didn't read the write up at all. He had details that matched what's in there."

"He could have read it before."

He could have. He did seem like he knew what book I had and what picture I was referring to before even looking at it. "That's true. But what are the odds?"

She rubbed her fingers across her chin. "Good point. But are you really supposed to believe something like that is possible?"

"I don't know, but if Joseph didn't believe Mary's story, where would we be?"

"So you think he's Jesus?"

"No!" I coughed. "That's not what I'm saying. I'm just saying sometimes you just have to believe in impossible things."

She uncrossed both arms and hoisted herself onto the desk, feet dangling. "So you think he's like a gift from God or something?"

"Not necessarily," I said, "but who knows? I'm just saying, anything is possible."

"Let me think about this."

"I mean, you thought he could be a ghost and he's not."

"What about an angel?"

I perked up at the idea. "An angel?"

"Yeah, why not?"

"Nah. I don't think so. He was cursed."

"But you said yourself anything is possible. And you said he was doing something good. The woman obviously thought she was helping him. Maybe she didn't mean for it to be a bad thing."

"I don't know." I shook my head pretty confidently that he was not an angel. I don't think angels are allowed to make out with people. Ugh, I shivered. "No way."

"If you say so," she said pulling her phone from her back pocket. "Oh boy, that's Jenna. We've got to go to breakfast. Her mom needs us to check in."

I glanced at the time. It was almost 9 a.m. "Yeah, we better go."

She finished telling me what little she knew about Erick Grant on the way to the elevator. Everyone was apparently hush hush and the only reason she heard anything at all was because of the twins' mom. We weren't really sure what to believe, or if it was even true. Until we got off the elevator. People from our school were everywhere, hugging and crying.

J. P.

Chapter 16

Giving Avery the okay to tell Rebecca whatever she wanted was an off the wall decision. But the truth was, keeping the secret for so long was wearing me down, and it felt good to get it off my chest with Avery.

There had been one other time that I had tried to tell someone else. And it wasn't for any reason other than I got lonely. A girl had taken to me one night, and she was pretty, like Avery, but she was also clingy. She spent every day, all day with me and I let myself confuse the attention with reality. She had seemed like someone who would want to stay in touch with me, so I let my guard down.

Instead of telling her where it all started in 1912, I

thought it would be better to lead in with the fact that I had to stay on the ships full time and couldn't really live on land. I didn't get passed that part before she started laughing.

The laughter stung and was a clear sign I misjudged my hope for reality. My life was some sort of joke and she'd never be able to handle it, even if she eventually took it seriously. I laughed back, telling her it was all in fun. She laughed some more and tried to drape her arms through mine, which I'd dodged and made some excuse to slip away. She didn't care to ask anything more about my past or connect the dots when I avoided her like the plague for the rest of the trip. I stayed guarded ever since, until Avery.

She'd peeled away the layers with determination and attention that was hard to resist. And if Avery trusted Rebecca, then it was her choice to tell her whatever she wanted. Plus, I doubted Rebecca would believe her anyway and then Avery could decide how to regroup from that.

After leaving the room, I went to the shopping deck and bought a few more shirts, underclothes and a pair of jeans that fit in my backpack. I hadn't planned on still being there, but by the way things looked, I'd need a couple more days of clean clothes.

I walked the halls for a few and noticed a definite change in the younger crowd. Most were texting a hundred miles per hour and taking turns looking at each other's screens. News was definitely spreading.

I ended up at the information desk, and before I knew it, the woman was leaning in, offering to help me.

I asked a few general questions about the upcoming events and directions to places on the ship which she obliged. I looked around after she was done talking and then pointed to the crowds.

"Hey, is something going on? I heard a bunch of high school kids talking about being scared and someone dying or something?"

"Oh it's just a class trip."

"What's going on with the class trip?"

"Oh you don't want to know."

I rested my elbows on the counter. "Sure I do."

"Well, a kid killed himself," she said slowly.

"Really?"

"Really." And she started telling me what she knew like it had been bottled up.

I was thinking of other questions when Scumbag walked by, sizing me up. I waited a few strides and casually followed him into the main dining hall where several gazes turned our way from dozens of packed tables. He walked to the right and I looked around to the left. Avery and Rebecca were sitting at a high table against the window. The twins were sitting at a larger, nearby round table with a blonde, short-haired woman.

I maneuvered around some chair backs to get to her. When she glanced over her shoulder and spotted me, she sat up a little straighter. I slowed my pace, unsure if I should interrupt, but her smile invited me to keep walking. When Rebecca saw me, she slid off the stool and sat one seat over, leaving me a space in the middle.

I sat between them taking notice of the ocean view.

"Everything ok?" Avery asked.

I looked at her and she was waiting attentively and then I glanced to my right and caught Rebecca staring at my chin, my cheek, shoulder, chest, hairline, pretty much at every detail she could see closely. And then she lifted her finger and poked me, lightly, in my arm and then once again, harder.

Avery leaned her head around me. "Rebecca, what are you doing?"

"Relax, I'm just curious," she said with her gaze still locked on my face. "Interesting," she murmured. "Well, you're real, that's for sure."

She was concentrating, thoroughly fighting a smile, clearly having been told the story.

I blinked, trying to remember where I left off and turned back to Avery.

"I went to the information desk to look in to some things. The clerk told me that your friend Erick Grant was found hanging in his bathroom this morning."

"Oh my God," they both said in unison.

"And he left a note saying he was sorry."

"Sorry about what?" Rebecca asked. "Hung himself? How?"

I looked around to make sure there was still enough audible distance between us and everyone else. "She also said they believe it was a confession about harming the missing student which must be your friend Kate."

"Maybe he did," Rebecca murmured.

"He didn't."

Her gaze cut to me. "How do you know?"

Avery put her palm on my arm. "Because Rebecca, Kate Thompson was pushed overboard on Saturday and J.P. saw who did it."

"Wait, you're serious about that?"

"Yeah, that's why he was asking us what she looked like the other day. When you told us she was missing. He saw it."

"Really?"

I nodded.

"Well who did it?" she pressed, looking around.

I swallowed and paused, trying to slow the conversation. "It's not a good idea to say it in here." I turned to Avery, hoping for assistance.

She moved her hand to my back in a comfortable way that both claimed and supported me in front of everyone. "You can tell her. Rebecca you need to stay chill."

I let her palm travel in a slow circular motion, taking her in and every minute that led me to be sitting between not one, but two girls who knew far too much.

I shook my head, shaking off the absurdity and turned to Rebecca. "I saw one of your teachers do it."

"What? Which one?"

Avery leaned around my shoulder. "It was Mr. Wells."

Rebecca's gaze darted around the room. "Sweet Mother Mary."

"Don't look!" Avery hissed.

She turned back, her eyes panicked. "What about Erick Grant's note?"

I shrugged. "I don't know about that, but he didn't kill that girl."

"We have to *do* something," she said.

"No, you don't," I said.

"Why not?"

"Because he's already killed one person, and could very well have something to do with the other."

Her eyes widened. "You think he killed Erick Grant too?"

"I think you should stay away from the scumbag."

"Scumbag? He could be a murderer."

I turned away to avoid going deeper into the conversation. The horizon had turned dark, much too dark for morning.

"We have to do something?" Rebecca continued.

Avery had followed my gaze to the horizon. It was unknown if she noticed what I saw, but she didn't say anything. Then she blinked. "Rebecca, I want to help, but I can't get involved. You know I need to lay low."

Rebecca nodded. "Then *I'll* do it."

"You'll do what?" Avery asked.

"I'll see what I can find."

I shook my head. "There is nothing to find. Just stay away."

"There *is* something to find. Mr. Wells told people that Kate was texting him that she was ok for three days. And Avery said she was texting Erick last night. But if J.P. is right, then she wasn't texting anyone."

Avery sucked in a breath. "Oh my God. I didn't think about that."

I exhaled and tilted my head back, not liking where this was going.

Rebecca slapped the table. "That means whoever did it, has her phone."

"And?" Avery asked.

"And if we can find it, then we can prove who did it. Wait, let me look up something."

Rebecca started searching her phone with pressed lips and urgency. After a few moments of searching and scrolling, she stopped a page with her finger and started reading. Her lips were moving with the words as she read. Avery and I watched her closely, wondering what she was doing when her lips froze. She dropped the phone like a hot potato and covered her mouth.

"What?" Avery asked. Rebecca slid the phone over to us. There was an article with the headline: "A Teacher On Her Honeymoon Goes Missing At Sea." We leaned in closer and zoomed the screen to read. There was a picture of a young woman at the top. Brown hair, looked a lot like an older version of the Kate girl. Nine years ago, she had been honeymooning on a cruise and went missing. She was declared dead six months after unsuccessful searches, assumed to have fallen overboard after a late night solo stroll. Toward the bottom, there was another picture of her with her husband, their very own Mr. Wells.

I slid the phone back not wanting any part of it. Avery looked away, and it was clear Rebecca was losing her cool. "I said I'll do it."

"Do what?" Avery urged, looking back.

"I'll find evidence. I'll look through his bags or whatever, in his room."

"This is really serious," Avery said.

"I know, which is why we have to stop him. Looks like he may have had some sort of obsession with look-a-like Kate. If he did this, we can't let him get away with it."

"You can't get into his room Rebecca. That's a crazy idea."

"There has to be a way."

They watched each other for a long time, and then I cringed, opening my mouth, just thinking about the scumbag.

At this point, I figured Scumbag knew I was a threat, and now Avery and her friend were also just by association. Which meant he was in a corner. And animals backed in a corner were unpredictable.

If I left either of them to their own planning, I was pretty sure it would be more dangerous than if we controlled the situation. Even if it was a bad idea. I sighed.

"I can get you in."

"Really?" Rebecca perked up.

"Wait. I don't know about this. How?" Avery asked, doubtfully.

"I should be able to get a key, the same way I got the information."

Avery shook her head. "I don't like it."

"Me either," I agreed.

"It'll be fine. I'm doing it," Rebecca declared.

"So what am *I* supposed to do?" Avery asked.

"You stay here," I said plainly.

She looked at me sideways. "And do nothing?"

Rebecca started gathering her napkin onto her empty plate. "You can make sure Mr. Wells stays occupied while I look. And just text me if he goes to his room."

"No," I said, not wanting her anywhere near Scumbag. "I saw how quickly he acts."

Avery didn't even look at me. "I can do it Rebecca."

"No." Now they were both tidying up.

"If she can go sneaking around his room, the least I can do is keep an eye on him. I'm doing it."

Her gaze did not waiver and she slid both of their empty plates and silverware to the edge of the table. She gave me one final stare.

"Okay, fine. Just stay away from the decks," I said getting up.

"And the bathrooms," Rebecca added, hurrying after me.

"Wait." Avery called, from her seat. "Don't forget your phone."

How in the world would Avery text her a warning if Rebecca left her phone sitting on the table. This plan was already failing. I shook my head as she went back.

"Hey, I got this," Rebecca said, catching back up. "Just dusting off the nerves."

"If you say so."

"Trust me."

I was doing a lot of that lately. On our way out, I took one quick glance over my shoulder to find two people watching me. The boy Avery had argued with and, in the distance behind him was Scumbag. I gave both of them a long stare, without breaking stride before turning back around with a smirk. After decades of adversity, I'm pretty sure my glare is intimidating, and at least I was getting to irritate two people who deserved it.

Rebecca waited by the elevators while I struck up conversation with the clerk. She was eager to flirt with me again, but getting her to break the rules was a little harder. She told me that security was already looking into it and that she could lose her job. I had to be honest with her, drawing her in on the investigation. I steered her to the web article about Scumbag and told her that we didn't think the kid killed himself and that my friend was just looking for a missing phone. She was just as taken aback by the article as we were. I told her if the school found out, that Mr. Wells could cover his tracks before we found anything.

After thinking a moment, she looked up at me. "That guy always creeped me out."

"You have good instincts."

"Thanks," she said, typing in a bunch of things. Within a couple minutes, she handed over a programmed keycard.

I walked Rebecca to the elevator. "Give me twenty minutes," she said, stepping aside.

"Twenty minutes," I warned as the elevator closed.

Back at the café, Avery had moved tables so she could keep a better lookout. I sat down with my back to the room, giving her a view of the room over my shoulder as we talked.

"Did you get it?"

"Yes."

"She just gave it to you?" Her brows were creased. "Why?"

"I showed her the article and told her we wanted to do some checking around. She was cool with it."

"Just like that? She must really be in to you."

"Maybe."

She rolled her eyes.

I tried not to laugh and diverted my attention to the horizon again. Even in the distance, the darkness was getting thicker.

"What is it?"

"It's about to storm outside. Looks like a big one."

She turned her head, scanning the view just over her shoulder. "Is that what that is?"

"It'll be here in an hour or two."

She shuddered.

"What? You don't like storms?"

"Not on a boat."

"You have nothing to worry about."

She fought a smile, and then as quickly as it was forming, it ended. "Crap, where is he?"

I slid my knees from under the table and fidgeted with my backpack to discretely scan the room. Scumbag wasn't at the bar and he wasn't where I could easily see him.

"He's leaving," she said standing up. There goes discrete.

She was headed around the table faster than I could close my backpack and catch up to her. "Slow down. You're being way too obvious."

Her voice cracked. "He's going back to his room."

I put my arm around her to slow her down. "Avery, it's a big ship."

"He's going, I know it."

"Ok, slow down. He can't know you're following him."

"Ok. You're right. Oh my gosh. What do we do?"

"We calm down."

She pressed against me and was shaking against my side. "I'm sorry. It's just if he's really guilty, this is bad."

"I know."

We hit the lobby and spotted him at the elevator. Several people were waiting to get on, and he was at the front of the pack, checking his watch. Just as he glanced our way, I shifted us behind a large pillar. Avery was nearly hyperventilating. Gone was the girl, unphased by the abnormal. She was in a panic for her friend, fumbling to hold her phone steady. "What floor is he going to?" she asked, trying to rotate it right side up.

I peeked around the pillar and saw the crowd filing onto the elevator. Several floor lights lit up. Making it too hard to tell which one he would have pressed.

"I don't know," I said. "There is a bunch selected. All going down." Most of the floors below us were the staterooms.

"That's it, I have to tell her." She hurried a text message saying *He's Coming,* and then she looked up to me. "He's going to catch her down there. It's not enough time. He'll see her."

I looked around, thinking. Again remembering what he did to the poor girl. How I'd tried to find her in the water. How she was gone. Just like that. Gone, and nobody even noticed until the next day. Rebecca was Avery's friend and she had guts enough to try to stop him from hurting someone else. So, I choked up the permission for myself to get involved again. "Listen, I'll take the stairs down and make sure she's ok."

"No you can't. He's already on to you."

"So."

"So, you know what he did to you last time."

I held her face still and lowered my gaze to get her to focus clearly. "And I'm standing right here. There is nothing he can do to me. You are another story. So stay here. Text Rebecca if he comes back. Got it?"

She nodded and I had to work fast. His floor was only four decks down and he had a head start. I hoped the crowded elevator would work in our favor. I hustled, keeping my head down, trying not to stand out too much against the people I passed on my way. If anyone got accused of room theft later, I was pretty sure it would be me. I reached the bottom and hurried to the corridor that turned toward Scumbag's room. Two adult men were lingering and conversing in the hall right outside his door. I cursed under my breath and hurried over to the elevator around the corner. I didn't own a cell phone, so the only way I could look casually distracted was to put my hands in my pockets and turn my back to the elevator.

When the bell chimed and the door opened, I turned around looking disinterested. Two women came out first followed by Scumbag. I glanced down the hall and no Rebecca and that meant she was still down the corridor.

Scumbag's eyes widened when he saw me, but he shifted around and turned toward his hallway.

"I've seen you somewhere before," I called.

He froze and turned back. The women kept walking. He sauntered up to me. "You have?" he asked, shifting his weight. The two men who had been around the corner, appeared and slid past us into the elevator.

"I have."

"Oh right. Yes, I saw you on deck with one of my students. Avery, I think it was."

"Is that her name?"

"I think you know her name," he replied, pulling his shoulders back.

"I talk to a lot of girls. It could be her."

"Right." His gaze followed along the ceiling as if he was calculating heavily. "How many do you talk to on the upper decks?" he asked, as his weasel gaze settled back on me.

"How many do *you*?"

He smiled, knowing he had the upperhand at the moment. "I have to run," he said. He turned away and then turned back. "Of course, it could have been your twin too."

While he was waiting for my response, Rebecca peeked her head around the corner and then tiptoed quickly down the hall and into the stairwell. I pressed the button on the elevator.

"I don't think so."

"Oh really? Why not?"

I stepped in just as close as when we'd met eye to eye on the upper deck that first night. Then, I spoke clearly, and slowly, so he wouldn't miss a single word.

"Because I don't have a twin."

And there they were, those icy eyes, the size of quarters. I exhaled a built up breath of tension and stepped sideways, into the elevator. Once the door closed, I paced back and forth, frustrated I didn't wring his neck right then and there. But as much as he didn't deserve to live, he deserved to die even less. To me, that was getting off way too easy. No, the scum needs to suffer. For a long time.

Avery

Chapter 17

It felt like forever before Rebecca flung open the stairwell door. She ran over and almost tackled me with a hug. I squeezed her back just as tightly.

"Oh my gosh," she breathed. "I was trapped in there. Mr. Hodge and Mr. Crowe were just talking right outside his door, so I couldn't leave. It felt like forever before they left. Oh. My. Gosh."

I pulled back enough to see her face. "Did he see you?"

"No, no. J.P. was there and kept him distracted by the elevator. I *just* missed getting caught. I'm so freaked out."

"It's okay. You're okay. Where is J.P.?"

She shook her head. "I don't know, he's still down there."

"Ok." I breathed in and out slowly. "It's going to be ok."

She spun me around. "There he is!"

J.P. was coming off the elevator. We hurried over to him and he quickly led us off to the side. "Let's go somewhere else."

"What happened?"

"Nothing, but he knows it's me who saw him with Kate."

"How?" Rebecca was trailing behind us.

"Because he was fishing for information about my twin, and I told him there wasn't one."

I swallowed a lump. "Why would you do that?"

"Because I had to distract him longer than I thought. *And* I want him on edge. Preferably the edge of the boat."

"But, he's a crazy person. He doesn't need to be provoked!"

"It's fine."

"No it isn't."

I turned to Rebecca. "Did you find anything?" She was biting her lip, and her eyelids were frozen like a statue. "Rebecca?"

J.P. guided us further into an unoccupied seating area with another massive ocean view. J.P. took it in for a moment and then looked back to us. Rebecca sat and exhaled. After a long breath and a good look around the empty area, she reached into her pocket. Her fumbling fingers slid out a tissue folded around a phone.

Our gazes locked on it. I hoped it wasn't what I thought it was. "Rebecca?"

She looked at me, stunned. "I found this under his mattress. It's Kate's."

J.P. leaned his head all the way back. "Why would you take that?" he asked, looking at the ceiling.

"What was I supposed to do?"

"Leave it where you found it, for now." he replied.

"Leave it so he could chuck it in the ocean? No way."

"How do you know it's even hers?" I asked.

"Because," she turned it over to show us the I.D card stuck in the back of the clear case.

I covered my mouth, looking at J.P. We were both waiting for him to say something. Anything, but he just sat there with tightened jaws. "What do we do?" I asked him.

He closed his eyes and pinched his nose. "Let me think."

I looked around and saw some people walking by. They weren't paying attention to us, but the phone felt like it had a beam of light around it. "Rebecca, put it away," I murmured.

"Right. Of course." She wrapped it back up and slid it into her pocket.

By then J.P. had leaned forward resting his elbows on his knees. "Rebecca, what do you want to do with it?"

She looked at him. "I don't know. I mean, I don't know. I wasn't expecting to really find anything."

"But what do you want to do now that you have?" he asked.

She shrugged, thinking. "Turn it in, I guess."

J.P. shook his head. "If you want my opinion, you should wait."

"Why," I interrupted.

"Because he saw me down there and the clerk knows I had his keycard. He will just explain it away and point fingers at me. It will just raise doubt. And we don't even know what it has on it, or if his fingerprints are on there. So it doesn't prove anything yet."

"So what do we do with it?" Rebecca asked.

"You keep it safe."

She creased her forehead. "You want me to keep it?"

"Yes. Do not let a single soul know you have it. Keep it turned off, so it doesn't ping in your possession. And you have to keep your distance from Avery and me."

"Why would she do that?"

"Because, your so called teacher is on to me and my connection to you. He doesn't know anything about Rebecca being aware. If he thinks you two had some sort of falling out, then he won't think she's involved or suspect she took the phone."

Rebecca nodded. "I can do that."

"And I will handle him."

They were just planning like I wasn't even there. "Handle him how?" I asked.

"We wait until he cracks. And if he doesn't, Rebecca will have the evidence, and take it to the police when you dock."

"Why not now?"

"Because, there is a good chance the security here will release it back to the school. And then that means-"

"Her chaperone," Rebecca said.

I turned to her. "Are you sure you want to do this?"

"Yes, I'm sure."

J.P. leaned back in his chair and let out a deep breath. "Okay then. It's settled for now. But you should probably go before he comes back up. I'm sure he knows it's missing by now."

She nodded again and I stood to give her a long hug. She hugged me back firmly, but gently like she always does. She always made me feel relaxed and never asked too many questions when I had something on my mind. With her, it was like we spoke an automatic language of understanding but no matter how much I liked her as a friend, she took me by surprise at how brave and determined she was. Always willing to support me and to do what was right for others. "I'll see you soon okay?"

"You got it," she winked and walked off toward the elevators. Afterward, J.P. told me he was going to grab us a bunch of food for my room and would meet me by the lobby, so we went our separate ways too.

Just outside the café, I caught sight of Mr. Wells coming off an elevator in a hurry, just as Rebecca slipped into the elevator next to it. I pretended to read my phone as he walked by. He stopped at the clerk's desk for several moments. The clerk was shaking her head several times with a few shrugs in between.

I went far enough to still see while sitting in one of the velvet covered lobby benches. He was jerking his hands now and a security guard came over and said a few words. After waiving his hands a few more times, he calmed down and the security guard backed off. A couple of teachers walked over to him and he shook his head and nodded calmly, settling down. His body language changed immediately. They eventually laughed in conversation and made their way through the outside deck doors, beyond the desk while Mr. Wells lingered.

A few minutes later, J.P. came around the corner with his backpack on one shoulder and a plastic bag. He saw Mr. Wells right away and attempted to walk against the wall casually and unnoticed. Mr. Wells spotted him quickly and walked up to him with his hands on his hips. After a moment exchanging a few words, Mr. Wells waived over a security guard.

They cornered J.P. against a high table nearby. Then he tossed his backpack on top of it and the security guard looked through each pocket and all his items. The security guard turned back to Mr. Wells and shook his head, but Mr. Wells pointed to J.P. and they began talking again.

After a few seconds, J.P. emptied his pockets and pulled up his shirt, pivoting all the way around. Mr. Wells had his arms crossed but they dropped to his side when his gaze landed on J.P.'s perfect skin, as if the four- day-old stab wound never existed. Although I was too nervous to smile, J.P. had a smirk on his face.

When the security guard seemed satisfied, J.P. started repacking his clothes and bags of food. The fact that Mr. Wells was clearly accusing J.P. of stealing was unsettling. If he was caught with the phone, it would be obvious it was Kate's. The only reason Mr. Wells would attempt to catch J.P. with it in front of security meant he was going to openly connect J.P. to it somehow. Now Mr. Wells was stumped, and as guilty as they come.

They let J.P. walk away, and instead of walking my way, he went toward the stairwell on the opposite side of the ship. I took that as a sign to distance myself, so I looked away and made my way over to the twins after spotting them.

They told me the ship was heading back to port and that Erick was in the ship's morgue. They were so rattled, they were literally shaking. "It's going to be ok," I said.

"Our trip is a disaster," McKenna moaned.

"I know," Jenna said, tears welling up. "I can't believe they actually have a morgue."

"You never really know people," Jenna added. "Erick. I mean it's crazy that he would do something like that."

"I know, right?" McKenna breathed.

I looked away, surprised they would think that so easily, but why would they think any different?

Mr. Wells was on his way past, checking his watch. I'd made myself seen casually enough with others, so I headed toward my room. "I'll see you guys later."

Just as I was reaching the stairs, Rebecca came out. I didn't have a reaction prepared, so I stopped in my tracks. She brushed right past me.

"So what? Are you actually going to hang out with us now?" she quipped, loudly. I looked back to her, embarrassed. She was waiting with wide eyes. "Are you? Or are you going to keep chasing after your new friend?"

"No," I said.

"Right. Sure, whatever."

She walked away so rudely that it made me wonder if she was actually mad at me after thinking about stuff.

"Rebecca?"

"It's fine, whatever," she called. "I'll just see you when we get home."

She'd never talked to anyone like that so I caught on to what she was doing, and Mr. Wells had heard it all. She turned back and bounced her way over to the twins without looking back a second time.

I blinked and turned back, entering the stairwell alone, feeling the rush of my heart beating between my ears. I hurried down one half flight after another until I was five decks lower. I never slowed my pace for fear Mr. Wells was following me even though I was probably the last thing on his mind. For now.

I think, if nothing else, we had done a decent job keeping him off balance. But, being paranoid was natural for me. Never go anywhere alone and always look over your shoulder. It wasn't that concept that worried me now. It was the fact that, on this ship, there is just nowhere to run. And that was a scary thought.

When I rounded my hall, J.P. was waiting next to my door.

"I'm so glad you're here," I breathed, catching my breath.

He moved off the wall, looking past me. "What's wrong?"

"Nothing, I just saw Mr. Wells. Rebecca did a good job acting like she was mad at me for not hanging out with her. I'm pretty sure he bought it. I almost did. He just gives me the creeps."

I fumbled with my key card cursing under my breath at how unstable my fingers were today. He slid the card from my hands, swiped it, and calmly opened the door.

After setting his things on the desk, he turned to me and took my hands in his. He pressed my palms together and pulled me closer. His warm hands rubbed the outsides of mine, until my heart rate settled and my breathing slowed.

"Sorry," I murmured. "I just can't believe that guy. That two people from my school are really dead. By a teacher. And he's walking around. Looking at me. It's crazy. I just want to get off this ship."

His hands paused.

"I'm so sorry. That's not what I meant."

"No it's okay. I don't blame you."

"It's really not what I meant. I just want to get away from him."

I wanted to kick myself.

"Avery, it's okay." He kept rubbing my hands between his.

I leaned in closer. "It's not okay. It's not."

He put his palms on my cheeks with a soft smile that didn't reach his eyes. "It's okay. I'll be okay. And you'll be too."

I was still shaking my head. "It's not fair."

"Maybe not, but I'm hungry. So," he said giving me a kiss on my cheek that lingered, "I'm going to eat right now."

He sat down and began unpacking sandwiches, drinks and snacks as if nothing was happening.

"Are you not worried at all?"

He took a bite of a breakfast sandwich and chewed it slowly until he was ready to swallow on his own time. "I'm more concerned about being down in this room with no view of the storm coming."

"Wait. What do you mean?"

"It doesn't look good outside."

So now we're talking about a whole other issue. "But we're safe inside, right?"

"Being down here, makes us blind. And I don't like being blind on the ship."

"I do," I said, then looked around at the white walls that surrounded us. I'd rather not see, but he wasn't buying it.

"You don't have to stay down here with me, if you don't want to."

He dropped the last corner of his sandwich and looked up to me.

"You actually think I'd spill my oldest secrets to some girl on a boat I just met. Get involved with a murderer just to keep said girl safe, all because I'd rather be somewhere other than right here?"

My face was feeling flushed, but I still had my hesitations. "Look, I don't want you to feel obligated to watch out for me, is all. You should do what makes you feel safe too."

"Are you listening to a word I'm saying?" I nodded. "Then stop talking nonsense. I'm staying."

He held back a smile and twisted off the top of his water bottle and took a big sip.

"Let's go," I said.

His gaze found mine as he swallowed.

"Go?"

"Yeah. Up. With a view somewhere."

"Scumbag's up there."

"But I'm with you remember?" I winked.

He watched me for a moment, considering. Then he stood. "You'd go up with me in a storm even if you don't like it?"

"If you say it's okay, I'll believe you. And I'm not hungry anyway."

"Okay."

The minute we left the narrow space, I felt a strange air come over us. "What about Mr. Wells?" I asked. He took my hand and pulled me along.

"I don't want to worry about him right now."

The fact that he was out there somewhere made me feel unsafe, but I was glad not to be alone. He led me through several narrow halls and doorways to an empty sitting area on the lowest deck that still had a panoramic view.

The small atrium was enclosed with glass on three sides. We were the only ones in there and were able to take up the center, front loveseat and make use of a large, matching canvas ottoman. The sky had turned gray and the waves of the ocean looked choppy, and yet the boat felt perfectly still.

"How did you know this was here?"

"I have time to explore a lot."

There it was. That content, but not really content look. I leaned in closer to him. "It's amazing," I urged.

We watched the sky darken before our eyes like an eerie, ghostly scene and I suddenly started thinking of home.

"Can I ask you something?"

His gaze lowered. "Yeah, sure."

"Can you tell me what happens when we dock? I mean with you. What happens with you?"

"Can we not talk about that?"

"I want to. The twins told me the ship was headed back because of what's happening. We're going to be home a day early. It's important."

"You don't have to worry about me Avery."

"I'm not worried about you. I get it, you will be fine. I will be fine. But you said you'll be somewhere. And that means I want to know how I would find you."

"You really want to find me?"

"You think I'd listen to some crazy guy tell me his ageless secret, and then tell him *my* real name, oh and put myself in the middle of a murder mystery just because?"

He just watched me.

"Are you listening? I like you. Like, really like you." I turned forward and crossed my arms with a shrug. "But if you don't feel the same, I get it."

I waited longer than comfortable for him to respond when he eventually pulled my hand to his lap. "You're the crazy one," he said.

I nudged him and went to pull my hand back, but he squeezed it in place.

"You want to know what happens? Okay, I'll tell you. I'll get really sleepy to the point where I feel drugged and can't stay awake. I'll go somewhere quiet just to rest, and then I lose consciousness and wake up somewhere else. It's usually a ship I've been on or have thought about being on. Any time the ship is going outside of the curse radius, I'll start to feel it. That's if I don't die first. If I die, then the same thing once I lose consciousness."

He was gazing back out over the ocean again and I realized I hadn't blinked once. I cleared my throat, bringing his attention back.

"So by curse radius, you mean it's tied to this area, that we're in right now?"

He nodded.

"I'll find you," I said.

He gave me a soft smile that wasn't all that convincing, so I leaned over and kissed his cheek, lingering long enough to breathe him in. With my eyes closed, I would remember his scent for a long time. It was a hint of fresh ocean breeze with a taste of spice that swirled its way around my lungs and through my brain.

He weaved his arm under mine, resting his palm on my thigh as we sat watching the rain come in. As dark as it started to look outside, it couldn't have felt more calm sitting next to him.

We had both fallen asleep when my phone buzzed in my pocket. A couple of hours had gone by and it was a text from Rebecca.

Wells is being really weird. I've seen him talking to two different sets of people, and the men looked, creepily, just like him. It's so weird. What is he doing?

Are you following him?

No. Well, kinda.

Rebecca!?

Relax. I'm not following him. Just paying attention.

J.P. was reading along with me. "She needs to stop that. And stay away from him."
"I know," I mumbled.

Rebecca, stay away from him.

O.K I was just letting you know. He's being weird.

He is weird.

Yeah, but this is weird. I see like multiple versions of him now. It's more creepy. Where are you?

I'm with J.P. in a lounge watching the storm.

That's another thing. They want us in the café. No one is allowed on deck. Ms. Jane said we can go to our rooms. I told her you were in yours.

Thanks.

Sure thing. Stay safe.

You too.

I slid the phone back in my pocket. "What do you think he's doing?"

"I don't know and I don't care."

"But what about stopping him?"

"All you have to do is turn the phone in when you guys get home. And they'll catch the scumbag."

"That's your plan?"

"Yeah, my plan is for you both to stay away from him. And then turn in the phone."

"What if he hurts someone else?"

"I don't think he's gotten away this long by being reckless. He only has two more days to get away with it in his mind and then he's off the hook."

"Except he knows the phone is missing now."

"That is true."

I cringed and laid my head on his shoulder, listening to the rain beat against the glass ceiling. These just may be the longest two days of my life. And I would have been extremely glad about that if it weren't for the fact that I'd be back to looking over my shoulder for a murderer.

J. P.

Chapter 18

The bow turned toward the waves. An attempt to head back early to New York took us right toward the path of the storm. Going around it would have turned us sideways which was far more dangerous than heading right into it. And that's exactly what the captain was doing.

Although I personally liked the ride in heavy waters, I was pretty sure Avery wouldn't. Or anyone else who signed up for a vacation only ride. If the rough water didn't terrify them, it would most likely make them throw up, neither of which was on the top of my list to watch. I stood up, casually stretched and then extended my hand to a nodding off Avery.

"Come on, I think we should go back to the room."

Her gaze locked on my hand. "Why?"

"It's just a good idea."

She took my hand and stood, eyeing me closely while moving into my personal space. "Why is that a good idea? You said you don't like being blind."

"I'm not blind now. I know what's going on up here and now I'm good with being down there."

She looked around and the rain had begun to pelt the glass.

"Is something happening?" she asked, looking back to me.

"I'm just ready for a change of scenery."

"Really? Is that an honest answer?"

I watched her, head tilted and eyebrows raised.

"You want honesty?"

"Um. Yes."

"Okay."

"So..."

"So, this storm is about to cause some rough seas. The captain is steering us right into it to avoid capsizing."

Her big browns got wide. "Did you just say capsizing?" I nodded. "Are you serious? Could that really happen?"

"Not likely. But if you aren't used to it, it will get scary up here."

"But you're used to it?"

"Yes."

"So what happens?"

"A lot of rocking, back and forth. And the waves will smash against the glass up here."

"And you prefer being in a room when this happens?"

I shook my head on instinct.

"No?" she asked.

"No."

"So where would you usually be?"

I looked around, assessing the glass on three sides, the view of the choppy sea, the greyness of the sky. And then I turned back to her. "I'd be right here."

"Right here?"

"Right here."

"Ok then, so let's stay."

"That's a no." I began walking.

"Wait. Why?"

"I said *I'd* stay here. Not with you."

"Why not?"

"Because it's not safe."

"But it is for you?"

"Do I really need to answer that?"

"Yes."

"It's not safe for a person who can die."

"So you'd stay because you know you won't die?"

"What's with all the questions?"

She didn't back down, but her voice softened in a way that tugged at my chest. "I'm just trying to get to understand you." She shrugged. "I want to know how you think. Is that bad?"

"Okay. I'd stay because it gives me a rush. Makes me feel like I am going to die. And...I don't know..it makes me feel real."

Her gaze settled on mine and she stepped closer. "Then let's stay."

"So I can get a rush?"

"So you can feel real."

Her words hit me, but my urge to respond hit me even harder. "You make me feel real."

Her lips parted and there it was. The truth. She made me feel more alive than the storm would. There was no doubt about that. Her presence hooked around my brain and spread all over. One girl with two names. One girl who knew me. One girl who cared to know what I was thinking. I took her hand in mine and led her away from the pinging glass.

She squeezed her fingers in mine, but slowed me down. "Where are we going?"

"To your room."

"But..."

"Just trust me please. This isn't really a time to test the waters for my sake."

She watched me for a second, contemplating a long breath, but then she reached up onto her toes and kissed me, taking her palms against my face and pulling me closer. Her lips tasted sweet and real became an understatement to how she made me feel.

I let her kiss me with the full control she wanted and mostly because I couldn't decide what to do next. Part of me wanted to pick her up and the other just pull her close. I was at a complete fork in the road, so I just let her do whatever she wanted. After a moment, she pulled back and grabbed my hand again like the kiss to her was a normal occurrence with me. "Okay," she said. "I trust you know what you're doing. So, whatever you say."

I blinked and if it weren't for the lightning that lit up the darkening sky, I may have stood there studying her for another few minutes.

We started walking down the narrow halls toward the state rooms when her phone buzzed. She stopped.

"One sec. It's Rebecca." Her shoulders slumped as she read. "Crap. Ms. Jane wants us in the café. Right away."

"That's not a good idea."

She paused typing and looked up. "Why not?"

"Because it's in an open space. With tables and chairs. Not a good place for a rocking ship." Just as I'd said it, we felt a small tilt. "See? It's coming."

"But I have to check in."

"Why? What are they going to do if you go to your room instead?"

"Well, I have to at least warn them. They should go to their rooms too, right?"

It's not that I actually thought of just saving ourselves. Most likely it would just be some rocking back and forth and everyone would go about their business. But when you find someone who makes you feel the way Avery made me feel, everything is heightened, including danger that probably didn't exist. Protective instincts kick in and it doesn't matter if you seem paranoid. It just is what it is, and I didn't apologize for it.

"You can warn by text."

Without a second thought, she agreed.

She texted a few more minutes and shook her head. "She says to come. It's important."

"Important how?"

"I don't know. Rebecca just said it's important."

It had bad idea written all over it, but it was pretty clear by the puppy eyes she was giving me, that she didn't want to leave her friend hanging. "Let's make it quick."

Avery

Chapter 19

It was dinner time when we reached the café. Aside from the grey skies, and water-beaded windows, everything seemed completely normal. Rebecca was sitting with the twins and their mom. I didn't know whether to envy their safety or feel sorry for their lack of freedom.

Ms. Jane had an untouched plate of food pushed away for a notebook and pen which she was concentrating closely on. An empty table was open near the glass, so I took the initiative to head that way, not even realizing I was still holding hands with J.P. If it bothered him to be on full display with me, he didn't act like it.

When we passed the table, Rebecca started to stand, but then held still.

"Avery," Ms. Jane said, her gaze traveling to our interlocked hands. I felt the urge to separate, but J.P.'s hand remained relaxed, but locked in mine.

"Ms. Jane, this is my friend J.P."

She was now watching us over her reading glasses. "Your friend?"

I stumbled across a few reasonable thoughts when Rebecca spoke up. "Yeah, it's cool. She like totally knows his family from way back and they ran into each other here. Pretty cool."

"Really?" Ms. Jane asked. The twins were exchanging glances. "That's interesting."

"Yeah, it is, isn't it?" Rebecca asked, elbowing McKenna.

She blinked and sat up. "Yeah, I didn't know that."

"Well ok then. Why don't you take a seat, so I can get you up to speed?"

J.P. excused himself and settled in at an empty table twenty or thirty feet away. He sat with the window to his left and the view of the room to his right. He was fixated on the ocean view that was now just a dark grey backdrop, beyond the glass.

Ms. Jane marked my name off her list of whatever and told me we would be back home Friday which was a day early. She told us grief counselors would be available when we docked, and at school on Monday. She wasn't mentioning anything about Kate Thompson. Everything was about Erick's suicide.

I didn't dare ask about Kate for fear of drawing attention to myself. With two days left on board, we had to check in three times a day with our chaperone plus the nightly curfew check that moved to 9:00 p.m. We were also encouraged to stay in groups.

I stood to head over to J.P.'s table and Rebecca blocked my path. She wanted me to get a plate of food with her, and even though it was an excuse to talk, I was hungry.

To get to the buffet, we had to walk right past Mr. Wells' table. At a quick glance, he was also concentrating on a notebook and paper like the rest of the chaperones. There was nothing out of the ordinary, other than the weird feeling that crept up my neck as we got closer. Just as we reached his table, he glanced up and I looked away with a lightning fast blink. Rebecca elbowed me and started giggling obnoxiously loud.

I turned to her, watching her hold her stomach and continue to hack up fake joy. It was so ridiculous, that I laughed too. I guess we made up. As soon as we reached the plates, she shut off the laughter like a light switch.

"That guy creeps me out," she said. "Here, take a plate."

I took the plate, following her down the line, taking the opportunity to add some sharable items for J.P. I was adding some mozzarella sticks when Rebecca started talking so low, I had to get close enough for our elbows to touch.

"So, we have a problem."

"Okay?" I said as we side stepped to the fries. "What's going on?"

"Well, they searched our rooms."

I froze, holding tongs in midair. Thoughts of my personal things being violated naturally crossed my mind first, but they quickly shifted to Rebeccca.

"Why?"

"They said they were searching for drugs. Because of Erick."

"Who said? When?" I wondered how on earth I missed that news.

"I found out from Jenna. Her mom told the twins it was going to happen."

We had reached the edge and she added a couple chicken strips to both of our plates. "I didn't think anything of it until she said Mr. Wells was in charge of it, then I bolted back to my room and grabbed the phone." She was whispering as we took the long route back to our table to avoid Mr. Wells.

"Oh my gosh," was all I kept saying.

"And then I just went into overdrive. I had to think."

"I'm sorry Rebecca. We shouldn't have put you in the middle of that."

"No, it's ok. He can't get away with being a psycho."

"So where is it?"

We were getting close to her table so she hurried her words.

"I had one of those fake books with a block carved inside to keep money and stuff in. I stashed it in there, and then asked Ms. Jane to put it in her bag that she always carries." I looked at her, stunned. "She doesn't know what's in it. She just thinks I got tired of carrying it around."

We'd reached the table by then and the floral quilted satchel was sticking out like a sore thumb, hanging in plain sight on the back of her chair. I had thought about making small talk before making my way back to J.P. but after hearing that, I told Rebecca I'd talk to her later and made a b-line over to J.P.

I sat the plate down and plopped quickly next to him. He looked at the plate.

"Hungry?" he asked me.

I pushed it more toward his way. "It's for both of us."

He raised a brow and grabbed a fry. "And you're thoughtful too."

He took a bite and I hit him with what Rebecca told me. He paused chewing for a second and then continued as usual. I waited, noticing a slight shake of his head. Then he picked up a chicken finger and held it up to my mouth.

"Did you hear me?"

"I did." He pushed it a little closer, and I took a bite, just so he'd put it down.

"And?" I asked, chewing.

"And, I told her this was a crazy idea."

"It was your idea for her to hang on to it."

He dropped the strip onto the plate. "True."

"So what do we do?"

He shifted my way, positioning my knees between his. "Your friend is a very smart girl. Trust that she knows what she's doing."

"She just gave the phone to a chaperone."

"The last place Scumbag would look for it."

He picked up another fry and put it to my mouth. I was so stunned, I took a bite to think. He put the rest in his mouth like we were just having a casual lunch.

I wanted to be sick and he was offering me another fry. I pushed it away this time, and he rubbed my leg and slid the plate away from both of us.

"It will be fine. She'll get it back and no one will know the difference."

"I don't like her having it. It's putting her in danger."

"Do you want me to go ask for the book? And then it will be on me."

I grabbed his hand in mine. "That's it. I'll go ask for it."

"Let me repeat. I can go ask."

I shook my head. "No, that wouldn't make any sense. They wouldn't think twice about me asking."

His gaze traveled toward the window as he was considering, but then his jaw tightened and his hand tensed up in mine.

Just toward our left was a darkening horizon that was higher than the ship. I'd watched the horizon in awe every morning, and not once did I see it as high as it was then. I didn't know what it meant, but I knew it wasn't good.

J. P.

Chapter 20

She squeezed my hand tightly, like she knew what was coming. I'd estimated we were about five minutes out from a really high wave, but I knew getting through it would be rough. Plus, we were positioned a little toward eleven o'clock, and even though the sheer size of our ship had handled the rough seas so far, I knew the captain had his hands full.

"We have to go."

"Go where?" she asked.

"The safest place," I said, "Is a small place."

She looked at me. "Like my room?"

My instinct was to say no, but for her sake, the room was probably the best place. It'd be far enough away from Scumbag, and the screaming chaos that was about to start.

"You know what?" I said, "That sounds good to me."

She squeezed my hand again and nodded. Everything about her wrapped itself around my chest and pulled tight. I wished she could stay with me forever, in any other circumstance.

Just like that, I no longer thought about myself first. Everything she'd wanted became something I wanted too.

"You should tell your friends they'd be safer in a small area too."

That's when her eyes got a little watery. "Is it that bad?"

We heard the sound of our porcelain plates sliding a few inches on the table, and she turned her attention quickly to her friends who were in the middle of a crowded room. Naive laughter could be heard at first shift, but the adults' faces were noticeably more serious.

Avery hurried over to Rebecca's table with me in tow and relayed the message that I knew was important to her. The woman they called Ms. Jane closed her notebook and put it in her bag.

"We've been told to all stay together," the woman warned.

Rebecca watched me. "If J.P. says we should go, we should go."

The lady looked at me too. "Am I missing something?"

I shook my head, "No ma'am. We're just in a rough storm and being in a big room like this could feel more unstable."

The two twins grabbed each other's hand and looked around. Several crew members had started collecting plates from tables. "By the way," Avery said, "Do you have that book I wanted to borrow?"

Rebecca coughed into her fist like she was having difficulty swallowing. She glanced at me and I tried to hide my shock, but my nostrils flared a little anyway. I looked away to hide my frustration.

"Are you sure you want it now?" Rebecca asked.

"Yes, I do. Can't wait to read it," Avery answered without hesitation.

"Okay. Ms. Jane do you still have that book I gave you?"

I turned back to see the woman reaching around the back of her chair to slide her bag off.

"Sure." She took it out, studying the cover closely. "What's it about?"

She put her thumb on the edges to open it. Rebecca's hands snatched it quicker than one blink.

"Just stuff. Here Avery." She practically shoved it at Avery's stomach.

Avery cradled it against her chest. "Thanks, you ready?" she asked, looking at me.

I was ready five minutes ago. "Most definitely," I said.

"See you later," Rebecca urged.

I pulled Avery's hand and started leading her away. A crew member had stopped to grab a wall to balance a tray full of dinnerware. We needed an anchor soon. A few feet away was a square pillar, and I maneuvered us on one side, and held still.

Avery was about to speak when I just told her to hold on to me. Plates crashed and several screams came before we really felt it, but when we did, she wrapped herself in a complete hug, pressing the book she was holding between our chests.

I wrapped one arm around her and held the pillar with my other arm. The floor tilted toward the pillar first, pressing her completely against me, her feet nearly off the ground. Tables and chairs slid past us with people trying to hang on to anything they could reach.

More plates crashed to the floor. Avery pressed her face against my chest and squeezed her arm around me. The book dug into my ribs but I held onto her even tighter. As the ship swayed back, close to even, I shifted us around to the opposite side of the pillar and held on as we lifted back up, in the other direction.

All the tables and chairs slid back across the floor, many turned over. People were rolling, sliding and screaming. One waiter's eye was cut and another was bleeding from his nose.

"We can't stay here," I said, urging her to look at me.

Her eyes were glassy and panicked, but she nodded.

"On the count of three, follow my lead." She squeezed me even tighter, making sure I wouldn't let her go. "One... two...three."

I pulled us quickly over to the exit. She never took one arm from my waist or the other arm from the book. Outside of the café, I grabbed another pillar and we held on during two more floor shifts. We could still hear more screams from inside the cafe. The crew was staggering around, trying to direct people to stay calm even though, those not anchored to something were tumbling off balance and rolling across the carpet.

On the next break, we hurried to the stairwell. I placed her one step in front of me as we both gripped onto the railing. We began making our way down each floor, one at a time, swaying with the boat and holding on tightly. Once we got inside the smaller space, it was much easier to steady ourselves, but several people clung onto the railing completely unwilling to continue up or down the stairwell.

When it felt stable, I took her and quickly moved around each clinging person until we could anchor ourselves back to the railing. Our hips pounded into the steel every time the ship would sway back toward it, so we moved as fast as we could between shifts.

A couple floors down, we came across a young woman sitting on a step. She had one arm looped through the railing and the other one extended out holding on to a stomping and crying toddler. When the boat gave a window of opportunity, we maneuvered around her and that's when we saw the infant she was also clutching in her lap.

"We can't leave her," Avery said.

"I know," I agreed. "Hold on."

I latched Avery's hand to the rail and just as I turned back, a tilt with just enough strength, rocked us all backward. The terrified mom's grip slipped from the little boy. His crying never stopped as he tumbled down three steps into my arms.

I pulled him up to my chest, bracing for each one of his hysterical kicks to my groin. I walked him unsteadily back to his mother. "Oh thank you!" she croaked, squeezing him between her knees. The toddler was still crying.

"Where are you trying to go?" I shouted.

"My room is two floors down, I think."

I steadied myself during another tilt and braced my leg against the boy in case he slipped free. There was no way she'd be able to make it on her own without one of them getting hurt.

"I'm going to guide you down. When I move, you move. Got it?"

She nodded. We worked our way down with Avery in front, me in the middle with the boy and mom close behind us with the baby. When we got to her floor, we continued down her hall and it took more effort to stay upright. The little boy clung to me for dear life. Just as we neared her room, a man came out in a hurry and embraced his wife.

"What happened? I was just coming to look for you!"

Avery was smiling as I handed over the boy and I had to admit, it felt good helping someone out. Afterward, we made our way down three more levels to her room.

I was physically exhausted.

Avery

Chapter 21

We had no idea how bad it was outside once we got to my room, but J.P. said it would be okay. He'd been in a lot of storms, so I felt safe with him. He was so calm, and he had held such a cautious grip on me all the way down to my room. Even still, my emotions were all over the place.

"What's wrong?" he asked, closing the door behind us.

"Everything," I quipped.

"I mean, are you hurt? Nauseous? Anything?"

"No, I'm fine, actually." I didn't want to let him know my nerves were a mess.

"Are you sure? You want me to stay?"

"As opposed to leaving? Why?"

"Privacy. I'm not going to assume."

"Assume what? That I want you here?" I was getting worked up because the last thing I wanted was to be sitting in my room alone. I crossed my arms, in a half pout, half challenge for him to read me better than that.

"Okay, relax." He held a raised brow. "I was just asking."

"Well, I want you here," I relented, turning away to slip off my shoes so he couldn't see my flushed cheeks.

I was the oldest in my family and forced to learn how to gain control of my life, and my own safety, way sooner than most people. Every decision I'd made had to be a smart and calculated one. And it was a control I'd learned to like and appreciate, but J.P. was in complete control, whether he intended to be or not.

It was well before curfew but was getting late, and that reminded me of school. I finally checked the book and the phone was in there tightly wrapped in a paper towel. I closed it quickly and slid it under the mattress. It was an obvious place, but the mere fact of having it out of sight made me feel better. Like I wasn't in possession of a murdered girl's phone.

J.P. sat on the foot of the bed and was discreetly flexing his hand. I walked over and laid it palm up in mine. There were angry looking red marks in his left palm.

"Oh my gosh. When did you get these?"

He pulled it back and made a fist. "The pillars. It's fine."

He held us balanced on those square columns for so long that his hand looked like it had been through a rodeo.

"I'm so sorry," I offered, sitting close to him.

I could still feel slight movement beneath us but it didn't bother me anymore. Not sitting next to him. There was just a senseless sense of wholeness. Maybe that's not the right word, but when you can touch someone or just sit next to them and feel a complete feeling of warmth all the way to your toes, there's no other way to describe it. It just was. We were both gazing at the floor. I sat, actually wondering if he felt the same things.

"Does this feel weird to you?" I asked.

"Weird how?" he answered, still looking at the floor.

"Weird, like I've known you more than a week. Like I don't know...like intense weird feelings just sitting here."

"Feelings?"

"Yes, *feelings.*"

We sat in a long silence and he checked his palm over and then closed it once again, resting it in his lap.

"I have feelings," he eventually replied, "And I don't like it."

My head turned his way pretty quickly, studying him.

"You don't?"

He turned to face me, his expression somber as he took a deep, long breath. "No."

"Why not?"

"Because you'll leave, and I'll still be here."

And in his eyes I saw the source of the warmth in my stomach, and there was no answer for what he said. No solution that made any sense beyond that moment and it was that exact moment in time that mattered to me and maybe even more to him.

I forgot about everything and leaned over, pulling his warm cheek toward me. I kissed him, silencing any questions either of us could have at that moment.

Without realizing it, my whole body was leaning into him and in a natural move, he wrapped his arm around my waist and gently pulled me the rest of the way onto his lap. We kissed heavily until he broke away and buried his face against my chest, holding me closely with both arms.

I let him lean into me with my cheek rested against his hair. I didn't know what to think. What it meant, being frozen in that embrace, but it spoke every bit of comfort, safety, need and fear all in one. Thinking about it, it was what I imagined falling in love to feel like.

I smiled and all the questions of the prior moments were gone. The next couple of hours went by pretty smoothly in the cabin as we lay in silence. Rebecca had texted that she and the twins made it back to their rooms. All the chaperones sent messages that we were in a mandatory lockdown, which made me happier to know other people would be safer from more than just the storm.

Rebecca and I continued to text back and forth while J.P. took a shower. A couple of students had gotten some bumps and bruises. Another had gotten glass shards in a knee from broken dishes.

It got tiresome with how long the texts were, so she decided to step out of her room to call me so McKenna couldn't overhear.

She was talking a hundred miles per hour. By the time J.P. was done, I had the complete rundown of everything and she was telling me how glad they were to be on lockdown, because she had seen enough of Mr. Wells.

As soon as we hung up, J.P. plopped down onto my bed, tucking his hands under a pillow and rested his face on the white fluff. I felt like doing the exact same, but needed a shower too. I set my phone on the table and grabbed some clothes from my bag.

I had a feeling Ms. Jane, or worse, Mr. Wells would come checking on me and I wouldn't be able to hear. I flipped over the interior security latch before going into the bathroom to make sure no one could just come in.

My shower was a good time to clear away the worry, uncertainty, and fear. Anything that would make me have less than a comfortable night sleeping. Everyone should be safe in their rooms. The storm was over. It was a good night. After the shower, I put on a long sleeve fitted Henley with some lounge pants, and tied my wet curls in a high bun that would dry later.

J.P. was still in the same position, but as I neared the bed, he lifted his head and rolled to his side. He looked really tired so I didn't want to bombard him with more conversation.

Instead, I picked up my phone and lay beside him. After scrolling through to see no missed calls or texts, I slid the phone to the bedside table. I rolled to face J.P. who was watching me with heavy lids. It was only 10:30 and I really didn't want to waste the night away sleeping. But once I rested my head under the crook of his arm, the day had finally taken its toll on me, too. My eyes closed to no thoughts behind them, and I fell asleep easily.

The next thing that woke me was the sound of my phone buzzing across the nightstand. I picked it up quickly to silence the vibration. Rebecca's face glowed. Through squinted eyes, I read the time of 11:30.

The room was still so peaceful and dark, that I didn't want to disturb it by talking on the phone, so I declined it and slid it beneath my pillow. Just as quickly as it stopped buzzing, it started again. I silenced the call and exhaled with closed eyes. She always had a persistence that I liked about her, but tonight was not the time. On her third attempt, I declined it and rolled onto my back to text instead.

What is it? Can't talk.

A few long minutes went by before my phone buzzed once.

I need the book I gave you.

At 11:30? Why?

Just bring it to me, now. Please.

I glanced over at J.P. He was sleeping soundly.

"Which one?" I asked, wondering if this was about J.P. and the historical book still sitting on the desk.

Bring my book to deck eight Tiki bar. Bring what's inside and come alone.

What?

Bring the book alone or we are in trouble.

What are you talkin about?

Just do it, alone, right now.

This was crazy talk and didn't make any sense.

We have a curfew?

Which is why no one will see. Come now. Alone.

One thing she wasn't was reckless and meeting her on a top deck close to midnight was very reckless. I studied the text exchange several times, and it made zero sense and that bothered me. She knew I had the phone and that I was with J.P. Why would she want or need me to bring it to her alone?

My heart sank, realizing she might be in some trouble, or worse. We had just talked and she was in her room.

I sat up. No, she left her room to talk to me. Oh my gosh.

I wanted to wake J.P. but knew he wouldn't want me going anywhere with that phone. I bit my pinky nail down to a nub, trying to come up with a solution. It was a ridiculously insane idea, but there was no way I was going to sit there. I slipped quietly out of bed, slowly slid on my flip-flops, and tiptoed all the way out of the room with the book.

J. P.

Chapter 22

I lifted my head when I heard the latch click. The room was completely dark, except for the thin line of light cast under the main door. I waited for the bathroom light to come on, but there was nothing.

I was a little disoriented, but remembered Avery's phone resting on the nightstand. I leaned over, feeling for it on the table, but ended up finding it on top of her pillow. The time read midnight. I had been out like a light, and was glad she had woken me up.

I could sleep any time, but couldn't spend every night with her. Falling asleep had been a waste of time, but my body was tired.

A few more silent minutes went by and I became restless. I turned on the small track lighting on the headboard and sat up, looking around. At that point the silence started to hit me like a siren and I leaned forward, listening. There was no movement and then I bolted upright and shifted toward the bathroom door.

I knocked with the back of my knuckles. "Avery?"

The bolt on the main door was unlatched from the inside, and in one motion, I jerked open the bathroom door to find it empty.

My mind ran down several scenarios, all to fall back on no idea what she was doing. All I could think about were possible causes. I assessed the room for anything out of place when her phone buzzed and lit up.

The screen flashed her friend Rebecca's face and a notification window popped up showing a text preview.

```
Time is running out.
```

I lifted my head, thinking. What were the two of them up to? The text preview disappeared as I glanced back, tapping the screen too late to hold it there.

The black screen taunted me and I pressed the home button in defiance even though I didn't have the passcode. Shocked, the screen opened to her full icons. I was certain I'd seen her unlock her phone with her fingerprint several times, and there it was removed, and unlocked.

The first place I checked was her text message from Rebecca. Nothing answered my question so I scrolled up and read further. My annoyance grew, thinking about what in the world either of them would be doing this late at night with the dead girl's phone.

I exhaled a frustrated breath and lifted the mattress pad. The book was gone, but the girl's phone was still sitting there. I shook my head knowing there was no reason for her to return the book to Rebecca without the phone in it.

I thought about putting on shoes and going after them, but it made me feel obsessed and it was none of my business. I'd been living a few days in a fantasy world. I recoiled back to the fact, that these people were a passing moment in time. Every one of them on the ship. I'd spent a very long time mentally accepting that fact.

A large part of that was knowing passengers come and go like a passing storm. They may live or die, both of which I envied. In my mind, living, really living was nice.

But really dying was too. The in between was nothing I'd wish on anyone. So I stood there with Avery's phone in my hand, wondering what she was doing and who she was doing it with, when in reality it didn't matter one way or the other.

She was not a fixture in my life and interfering with hers, as much as I'd wanted to, went against every rule I'd made for myself. If she wanted to investigate the texts, then she could. If she'd wanted me to know, she would have woken me up. I sat back on the bed, making the decision to wait for her to come back, while convincing myself that she could do whatever she wanted.

Avery

Chapter 23

I'd taken off the lock screen to my phone as a way to let J.P. know where I was. I didn't want him to stop me from going, but I hoped with everything in my stomach that he would wake up and find it. I'd seen how protective he was by nature. It was just in his instinct to reach out to help people around him whether he wanted to or not. He'd shown it during the sinking. He'd shown it when he tried to step in for Kate Thompson and he'd shown it with just his concern for me and my friends.

Going out to meet Rebecca at midnight was completely off. She would never ask me to meet her and bring that book which meant she needed it for another reason. So I inched my way down a hall with no clue where to go or why.

I'd walked beside J.P. enough times to make me feel completely alone now. It was like I was a child who couldn't find their way. No one was around and yet it felt like a thousand people were walking right behind me, crowding my heels and blowing on my neck.

I shivered and looked back one more time to see an empty hallway again. Nothing felt right about the moment. I stopped at the floor plan on the wall. The Tiki bar wasn't listed, but there was some sort of bar area toward the front of the ship so I dragged my finger along the directions to get there.

I took the elevator to deck eight and made my way down a few empty walkways that led to a narrow hallway. Signs pointed toward the viewing deck. It was completely desolate, but the closer I got to the glass door at the end of the hall, the more I felt like someone was following me.

I looked back a few times hoping to see J.P. At that point I wanted him to come jogging up behind me. To tell me to go back, but the hall was completely empty. I hadn't even seen a single crew member, and I shivered with unease.

As I got closer, I looked around for somewhere to stash the book. My gaze settled on a door to a stairwell to my right.

I gently pushed it open to find it empty, too. I climbed one flight and set the book on the floor as a prop to hold the door open on the 9th floor. I hoped if anyone saw it, they'd leave it alone thinking someone was just using it to serve a purpose.

Back down on deck eight, I reached the glass door. It was completely dark inside. There was no sign on the door or any other reason to assume it would be locked, so I took a long, deep breath and pulled the handle open. I was immediately hit with a cool breeze and the whooshing sound of distant waves.

The large room reminded me of the observatory J.P. had taken me to earlier but this one was a larger room, possibly the width of the whole ship at its widest point. There were glass walls on two sides with the right side completely open to the outside. There were lounge chairs and tables I could barely make out in the darkness. As I walked, the floor was slick from the earlier rain and I had to focus not to slip. A little further into the room, I saw a person standing next to a pillar.

"Rebecca?"

A muffled sound quickly turned to a chilling high pitch, squealing cry and an arm wrapped around me too fast to react. A sharp object pressed into the side of my throat. I felt the blade dig into my skin and I squealed too.

"Where is the phone?" the voice asked, his breath in my ear.

I'd heard the voice lecture us for an entire year. A boring monotone that sounded oddly the same now, but the proximity to my neck made me cringe. I didn't want to acknowledge who it was, but something told me it didn't matter.

"Mr. Wells, what are you doing?"

He pressed the knife deeper into my throat. The sting felt like it would slice down to the bone if I moved too much. "I'm going to ask one more time."

"It's not that serious, okay? You can have it. You can have all our phones if you want."

"One. Two. Three."

"Okay, I hid it out in the hall."

Rebecca started mumbling some pleas.

"Take me and I'll get it."

"No," he said, pushing me forward.

As we got closer to Rebecca, I could see he had her hands tied around a pillar and her mouth gagged. Her eyes were moist and actively searching around for help, but we were alone.

"It's okay," I said.

"Shut up!" Mr. Wells barked. "I've had enough of this."

He quickly sliced through Rebecca's ties and put the knife back to my throat, the stinging in my skin returning.

"You," he hissed at Rebecca. "Go get the phone. Or say goodbye to your friend."

"So you can kill us both?" she asked, taking out her gag.

"I don't think you two will be causing me any more trouble. You'll have learned your lesson and will keep quiet. Now go get it now."

"No," she said, firmly. He dragged me toward the uncovered deck. "You have two minutes or she's over. Your choice."

"Okay. You can have it," I called out. "It's in the stairwell right outside on deck nine."

Rebecca shook her head and pleaded, "We can't."

Mr. Wells lifted me off my feet and turned me toward the railing. Salty wind assaulted my face and flew my hair around. I wanted to scream but the knife pressed into my skin. I closed my eyes.

"Okay, okay!" she yelled. "I'll go."

"One minute and she's over," he called as she backed away. "You have sixty seconds."

He set me down but kept the knife at my throat as Rebecca turned and ran. My gaze traveled down the railings. The white waves from the wake were splashing by several stories down. I cringed at how fast the ship was moving, the waves splashed past like white water rapids. The sounds of swooshing made every muscle in my body quiver. I squeezed my eyes shut again, thinking of what to do when he realized we didn't have the phone.

"Here!" Rebecca shouted, coming back into the room, cautiously walking toward us.

He pointed to the deck railing with the knife. "Over there," he ordered.

Her gaze followed, reluctantly. "Now!" he growled.

She hesitated, but walked to where he was pointing which was about 20 or 30 feet away from us. Her hair started blowing around as she neared the rail.

"Let me see the phone," he said.

She glanced over the edge and quickly back again, holding up the book. I tensed, fearful of my mistake, knowing an empty book would only make things worse for us.

"Give it to me," he said.

I opened my eyes to see her showing him the open book with a phone inside. My eyes widened.

"Here," she said. "Come and get it."

She tossed it onto the floor between us and to our right. "You can have the stupid thing. We don't want it." Her gaze traveled around nervously.

"You stupid girl. Never could follow directions." He took a frustrated breath. "It's time for you to go. Climb the rail and jump."

Her eyes narrowed. "What?"

"You heard me. Climb the rail and jump."

"No," she said, "Are you insane?"

"Have it your way." He lifted me again with one arm around my waist. The ocean waves became deafening.

"You or her," he threatened.

"Okay. Okay," she called, putting her hand on the railing. I could see them shaking.

Just seeing her about to hoist herself over the edge made me panic. Without thinking, I just took all of my weight and stomped both feet on the ground, and kicked myself backward. The momentum pushed me into him. As I held onto his arms, we both went flipping over the railing.

His hold on me released as we both plummeted against the wind. I heard screams and wasn't sure if it was my voice or Rebecca's.

Cold sea mist smacked my face the whole way down. We hit the water with a thud. I closed my eyes and held my breath as I smashed through the choppy wake. I was tossed and flipped around and pushed with the undercurrent. When I reached the surface, Mr. Wells was swimming over me, flapping his arms sloppily.

I swam back toward the boat but the current pushed me closer to him, swishing us around like a washing machine. He grabbed me, pushing me under. I didn't have time to take a breath before the water rushed in my mouth.

I kicked back up, coughing and gasping for air. His elbow knocked my chest and his palm covered my entire face, pushing me back under.

Sounds of water gushed throughout my ears, and somewhere in the distance, I thought I heard my name. Maybe it was all just a dream. I reached the surface again, long enough for another quick breath.

"Avery!" The voice shouted again. Too panicked for a dream.

"Help!" I croaked, as Mr. Wells pulled me down again.

Disoriented, I kicked back up. His body weight lifted as I reached the surface, coughing and choking on more water.

J.P. was there, grasping the back of Mr. Wells' hair. He yanked him backward and shoved him across the water with one huge shove.

"Oh my God," I cried.

"It's okay." He grabbed me by my shirt, pulling me until we were eye-to-eye. Water was smacking against the sides of our faces.

"Come," he said, swimming with one arm and pulling me with him.

He was guiding us away from the ship sideways. He paused when a large swell came and he clutched me around my ribs.

"Where are we going?" I gasped.

"Away from him and the wake."

"He tried to drown me," I croaked.

"He can't swim," he said, pulling me further.

"What?"

"He was flopping around like a fish out of water."

My mind was swirling. All I felt was pressure pulling me under.

"Okay, this is far enough."

He stopped pulling me and took his hand, moving hair out of my face. "Look at me." He turned, his gaze locked on mine. "The ship will come back. Just relax. I need you to relax and float with me."

He was talking calmly, but the death grip he had on my shirt was urgent. I nodded holding his arms.

"Easy," he said. "I don't want you to get separated, so I won't let go."

I nodded again, looking back at the ship. It was far now, and I couldn't tell if it was turning back or not. It was completely dark around us.

"What happened?" I asked.

Another swell lifted us up. "Woah," he mumbled pulling me back toward him.

"What do you mean, what happened? You jumped over the railing like a crazy person and took a crazy person with you."

We reached the top of the swell and lowered on the other side. I was clutching him for dear life. I was a pretty good swimmer, but we were surrounded by dark and I didn't even want to think about what was swimming around under us. I tried to refocus.

"I didn't have a choice," I said, more trying to convince myself than him.

"I was coming you know? When Rebecca brought back the book, I was there. She was trying to distract him."

Water splashed my face sending my hair into my eyes and a gush of water into my nose.
He pulled me back to him, again, and moved my hair so I could see. My hand still gripped his arms.

"I didn't know. I'm sorry, I just reacted. He was going to kill us both. I just wanted him gone. That's all."

He still had a tight grip on my shirt but he smiled. "I think you managed that."

"Where is he?" I asked, looking around.

"I don't know, but he's probably drowned by now."

Another swell came, pushing us apart but he held tight pulling me back. The thought of what I would do out here alone terrified me and I realized I was shaking.

"I'm so sorry," I said.

"For what? You're fine. Rebecca's fine. I'm fine."

"We're not fine. I've got us out here in the middle of the ocean. My legs are tired. It's all my fault."

"No, it's Scumbag's fault. And we're fine. The boat will circle back."

"It's not coming back." It was way too far now.

"It will. It's probably taking Rebecca a little while to find someone to tell, but she will. And they'll start the rescue process."

"I don't know if I can make it much longer."

"I can. Just stay with me. Let me know when you can't go anymore."

I nodded, feeling the burn in my thighs with each kick. As much as I tried to relax, knowing that was the best way to tread water, each ripple came with a splash of salt water into my eyes or my nose. There was nothing relaxing about it and I knew there was no way I could go much longer.

J. P.

Chapter 24

It had taken me about five minutes to figure out Avery unlocked her phone for me to find the messages. It took another minute to figure out she'd taken the book but left the dead girl's phone for a reason.

I'd taken Avery's phone with me as I hurried to the exact place I knew they were. Just as I arrived, Rebecca was rushing out of the glass doors shaking and talking to herself.

As soon as she saw me, she ran over, pleading, barely making any sense. Her eyes were wild and bloodshot. When she told me what was happening, I wanted to go in and wring his neck but didn't want to provoke him to throw her over like I knew he could.

I convinced Rebecca to get the book and put Avery's phone in it to buy us time. When she could, she was supposed to toss the book hopefully tempting him to go for it. I'd have been able to take him down when he was distracted.

It was working. I had made my way into the dark corner and when Rebecca touched the railing, he was completely focused on her. And then out of nowhere, Avery stomped both feet on the deck and launched them over.

It felt like I was running in slow motion. I shouted for Rebecca to get help and went in as fast as I could.

Since we fell toward the front of the ship, we had a minute of lighting until the stern passed our location. I saw him flailing his arms in desperation, trying to clutch onto something when I realized that something was Avery. I swam so fast.

I wanted to cause him serious harm, but worried more about separating from Avery in the dark current. I couldn't lose sight of her like I had the Kate girl. I snatched him by the back of his head and shoved him toward the wake of the ship.

As she clung to me now, I knew I wouldn't let her go. It would be at least 30 minutes before the ship could turn around and it could be hours before the rescue boat narrowed down on our location.

"So what will happen now?" she asked.

I could tell her kicks were more labored and infrequent.

"Relax," I told her. "Relax your body and float with me." The waters were too rough for her to relax on her back and float like I wanted her to but she still needed to try.

"What if they don't come back?"

"You think your friend would let them forget about you?"

I was holding back my smile until she giggled and then I laughed too. "See, you'll be fine. Just fine."

She let her smile linger and then looked around again. The ship was pretty far off still.

"I'm so sorry," she said, her eyes as glassy as the water in the moon's reflection.

"You keep saying that."

"Because I am. I feel so stupid."

"Don't. You took out Scumbag."

A slight smile returned but only for a second.

"It was a stupid idea," she said leaning her head back.

"Yes, it was," I agreed.

She pulled her head forward and shoved a splash of water at me with an open palm. When she let go, a wave pulled her to my left and it took both hands gripping her shirt to pull her back. The force of the wave pulled her under at the last minute and she didn't have much strength to kick back up.

It had been about 20 minutes treading in the rough waters.

"Okay, okay, you've had enough." I turned her away from me.

She tried to turn back. "What are you doing?"

"Relax, I'm going to hold you. You did good. Now you need to rest."

I pulled her to me so her back was against my chest. I wrapped one arm around her waist and under her shirt so I could grip it from the inside.

I kept us a float on my back using my free arm to help me tread.

"Relax," I spoke close to her ear. "I've got you."

After a few deep breaths, she began kicking gently in slow unison with me as we floated. Eventually, our bodies moved with the ocean. There was a sense of calm for a moment, but she started shivering even though the water wasn't that cold. I put my cheek against her face, generating warmth.

"Let's talk about something."

"Okay," she said, settling her breathing.

"So tell me why you like me?"

She laughed.

"I'm serious."

"I don't know," she said. "Why do you like me?"

"Who said I liked you?"

"Oh my gosh."

"I'm serious."

"Maybe because you jumped off a ship for me in the middle of nowhere?"

"I jumped off for the Kate girl too and I didn't even know her."

She paused her legs a moment. "Then I guess I really am sorry to drag you out here and all." She turned quiet for a while.

"So back to why you like me?" I asked.

"Are you serious?"

"Yes."

"Well I'm not sure that I do anymore."

"Why not?"

"Maybe because I don't like people who don't like me back."

"I never said I didn't like you."

"You kind of did."

"No, I didn't."

"My gosh." She started squirming to put some distance between us.

"Okay, okay," I pulled her back pressing her entire upper half against me, knowing her threat was a mute point. "I like you."

"Gosh stop antagonizing me."

"It's the truth."

"Then why are you being so difficult about it?"

"I'm not. I was just trying to distract you."

"From what?"

"From time. Look, the ship is on its way back."

I turned us around so she could see the growing light. "Oh thank God. Thank you. Thank you."

"See? It worked."

"Except I don't trust you now."

"But I'm saving your life right now."

"You're impossible."

"How so?"

"Because. I want to punch you but I can't."

"You can punch me."

"And risk drowning? No way."

"So you need me then?"

"Yes, I guess I do."

"And you like me?"

"Yes, I like you."

"Good, then we agree."

The tense muscles had relaxed at my words. They weren't anything special, but validation possibly for both of us. I got her to turn back around and rest, trusting that the ship would make its way to us.

We lay for several quiet moments. The swells were coming and going, but we were rising and falling pretty easily with them. The moon was high and if she weren't in danger, it would have been a great moment for me.

Another swell lifted up, trying to pull us apart. It was getting harder to hold on to her.

The boat had launched the rescue vessel and it was about a hundred yards off.

"Avery, you need to scream out for help so they can hear you."

"Okay."

"As loud as you can."

I put a little distance between us and she started yelling, "Help! Help us!"

"That's it. They'll see you."

I stayed quiet as she called out while a terrible feeling of regret crept up. Help would be there soon and that made me relieved for her. I'd wanted to make sure she didn't become Scumbag's next victim and I had done that. But the reality was setting in for me. She could go home now, and I realized in that moment that she could do it without any long goodbyes or making promises neither of us could keep. She had given me more life than I could thank her for.

The orange rescue boat was about 40 yards away and shining a spotlight toward us.

"Tell them my name was John. That's all you know."

Her body turned completely my way. "What do you mean?" Her eyes wide with a mixture of shock and confusion. Her hands nervously fumbled beneath the water between us.

"When they get you, tell–"

"When they get us."

"When they get you."

She clutched my t-shirt with both hands and I tried to pull back. "What do you think you're doing?"

"I can't go back there."

"What? Yes you can. What are you talking about?"

She clutched me now and I realized I'd let her go completely.

"I can't. Time is running out on that ship for me."

"No, it isn't!"

"Yes, it is."

"No, we haven't made plans. Or said goodbye. No."

"I don't want to say goodbye."

"Then don't."

The boat was right near us now.

"Here she is!" I shouted, then turned to look at her, holding her face in my palms. "You were the one." I took her hands and pushed off and let myself sink.

As I kicked myself lower, a sharp tension pulled at my waist yanking her with me.

Confused, I pushed her up and her body yanked back toward me, pulling sharply. We were under water long enough for me to worry, so I kicked upward, aborting, rummaging around for an answer.

When we reached the surface, she gasped for air while my panicked hands felt around. Under the water, my sweatpants' waist string was tied to hers. My gaze widened in shock, realizing what she'd done.

Two men tossed life rafts to us.

"Get him!" she shouted, pushing me toward the boat.

The two men grabbed and hoisted us up side by side. Still confused at what just happened, I laid on my back with my hands clamped over my forehead. Avery rolled completely on top of me with her face in my neck, clutching me like a teddy bear. Her words were muffled against me but I made them out clearly. "You're such a jerk."

Avery

Chapter 25

Four rescuers in yellow raincoats threw a heavy blanket over us. J.P. lay completely still with me on top of him refusing to move. Fear of him jumping over or something dumb kept pressing in my mind. I was overwhelmed with confusion and relief all at once. I could hear them talking over the radio, planning the next step. The voices were surprisingly calm and professional. As if a crazy rescue was routine.

They raised our boat on some sort of lift system and when we reached the top, they took a pocketknife and separated our attached strings. There were a lot of people huddled around and my body was hoisted onto the deck.

More blankets were added, and someone started checking my blood pressure. Through the group of medical staff, I could see Rebecca was there in the distance with Ms. Jane and Dr. Abney.

Out of the corner of my eyes, I saw someone try to put a blanket on J.P. He put a hand up and turned away. It looked like he was going to bolt and I was too exhausted to focus on it at that moment. If he wanted to leave that badly at this point, then so be it. I let the team warm me, check my pulse, my pupils, and anything else they needed.

When I turned back around, J.P. was gone. A tall, dark gentleman in a navy uniform with gold buttons, knelt beside me with a pen and pad.

"Miss, can you confirm your name?"

"Avery Monroe."

"And your friend's name?"

My breath caught as I looked around for him. "Where is he?" I asked.

"He went inside. Refused medical attention. His name?"

I blinked. "I don't know. John. That's all I know."

"John? Just John?"

"Yeah, just John."

He studied me a moment and then wrote a few letters on his paper.

I was taken to the infirmary and once given the all-clear, I was guided to the security office. They took a statement. Rebecca had already given them her story about Mr. Wells, who they were still looking for. Neither of us talked about the real J.P. and our stories matched. Rebecca had already started the passenger we just met story. Not knowing much about him other than he helped us when we needed it. It was vague other than our details of Mr. Wells, so they let us go.

Ms. Jane had stayed with me and called my mom for me. She downplayed most of the details, which I was thankful for. Then she walked me back to my room. I assured her I was fine and just extremely tired. She flipped my light on, satisfied I was safe and gave me a nice hug that I didn't know I needed until that moment.

She left and I latched the bolt behind her, more than thankful to be safe and back in my room. I was still wet and started taking off my shirt when the bathroom door opened. J.P. came out, still wearing wet clothes too and stopped in my entryway, waiting.

I was down to my bra and sweatpants and my hair was a salty mess. When I saw him, I rushed at him, pushing him backward.

"You jerk." I was chest to chest, challenging him. He backed all the way against the door. "Say something."

"Just calm down a minute."

"What were you thinking?" I pushed him again, so angry and unsettled and out of my mind with disappointment. "Was that going to be it? Just leave? That's it?" I pushed him again and he grabbed my hands.

"Stop it!" he said, holding me still. "I don't know. It just seemed like the right thing to do."

"The right thing? I've just been through a washing machine and you thought just drowning yourself in front of me would be the right thing? I can't even." I pulled my hand away. "Why would you do that to me? Why?"

"I'm sorry," he said, pulling me close enough to lean into him and I did, a little. I fought anger because I knew I'd been scared of what happened to me and also partly from knowing he almost left.

"I wouldn't have done that to you," I said.

"I know that now," he murmured. "I'm sorry."

I stood there against him but hesitant to fully lean in. His chest rose and fell calmly within the little space between us. I couldn't even look at him for fear of not knowing what to say. In the long moment of silence, I felt myself cool down and got a chill that caused my body to shiver.

"Come on," he whispered, reaching for the bathroom door.

He opened the small room and led me inside. My arms were crossed, both feeling exposed in the brighter light and to keep warm. He shifted me closer to the sink as he closed the door behind us. His movements were calm and casual at first. But then he turned and opened the rounded glass door to the corner shower.

Confusion grew as I stood there watching. He turned on the water, waiting, and feeling the temperature with his hand. My mind was questioning everything, trying to reconcile how I felt about him after he tried to disappear to now being confined in such a small space with him.

I thought he was going to use hot steam from the shower to warm up the bathroom until he pulled his shirt over his head with his back still turned to me. I prepared to turn around if he planned to get in, but he slowly turned toward me and dropped his shirt in the corner next to us. His dark eyes raised slowly from the floor until his gaze pierced through every thought of mine.

J. P.

Chapter 26

When I felt her shiver, I didn't want the moment of danger, or anger, to keep lingering. I'd made a dumb call in a moment where I didn't really think about the immediate consequences or the effect on her.

She challenged me in more ways than one and when it came down to it, I was going to bolt the first chance I got. And I would have regretted it, but that didn't mean it didn't seem like the right thing to do at the time.

She made me second guess everything. When the rescuers came, I convinced myself that her attachment to me was more self-preservation. And then she clung to me for no reason other than to keep me with her, and that worried me too.

In an instant my mind got all clouded again and I almost jumped back overboard when I had the chance. The confusion was deafening and I needed to sort out my thoughts.

A long walk took me back to when I felt lost and alone a long time ago with nowhere to go and no one to turn to. All I'd wanted back then was to go home. And home was impossible then and it was impossible now.

The closest place in my mind was to go to Avery's room and so that's where I ended up. Of all the places on the big ship, it was in her tiny room with no window that I felt home, even if not perfect.
I had no idea how she would have reacted and it didn't really matter. I just wanted to be there with her again.

When I saw her, I felt good, and when she got mad and took her anger out on me, I felt even better. Like I deserved it and needed her to push the negativity out of me. And standing there with her, it was gone. It was complete silence and in the quiet there was peace. It was a peace I'd give anything for as long as she wanted me to.

And when she shivered, all I'd wanted to do was hold her, but we were both wet and cold. I wanted badly to wash away the salty memory from the both of us.

After I turned on the shower and took off my shirt, I waited, not wanting her to feel cornered or uncomfortable. She watched me uncertain, but curious.

I wondered if she was going to move or say something, but she just looked at me. I stepped toward her slowly, watching her for a reaction. Her hair was down in messy wet curls, and with no make up at all, she was more perfect than any image I could possibly remember of her. I reached my hand up and softly touched her shoulder, and she leaned slightly into me. She was close enough to where I could no longer see her face.

My fingertips traced over the strap of her bra and I slid it down the side of her shoulder. She did not tremble or move in any way, so I let the strap fall and took my other hand to her other shoulder. She still stood waiting, her breath catching against my shoulder.

I moved the other strap and let it fall too. Without a word, my fingertips traveled over her shoulders and gently down her arms and onto her hips. She stayed close to me as my hands traveled around her back onto the hook of her bra. I held my fingertips there, waiting for a reaction or maybe even permission. She took one small step closer to me and my lips parted slightly. I moved my fingers and her bra fell to the floor between us. Her gaze met mine and her lips softened slightly, making me feel warm already. I took my hands and pulled my own sweatpants and boxers down to the floor. From there, I turned and got into the warm shower, giving her the additional privacy I thought she may want. The warm water hit my chest as I waited, hoping she would follow. There was a stillness in the air and I began to wash away the saltiness of having been in the ocean for an hour.

After a minute. I felt her step into the shower. She closed the door behind us and her cool body was close enough to mine to feel there was only a very small distance between us.

Avery

Chapter 27

The shower was so small that I had no choice but to stand closely behind him. My heart was ricocheting inside my chest, but I stood as still as possible, steadying my breathing. He waited a moment and then turned his body around, water dripping down his defined chest. My gaze traveled everywhere but at his eyes for fear of losing any nerve I was building up.

His hands touched my shoulders and he steered me gently until I was facing the glass. His hands tilted my head back, and I felt him shift to the side, so the water reached my hair. Once it was rinsed, he moved the hair around to the front of my shoulder and began to move the small soap against my back. Instant heat settled over me and the warm and fuzzy feeling in my stomach relaxed me so much, that my body leaned into him.

He moved the soap around to my chest and worked his way down my legs. I turned toward him, allowing the water to rinse away the smooth trails. His gaze focused on every aspect of my face. There were no more nerves. No more chills. And no more hesitation. Just an urge. I tilted forward, on my toes until our lips touched. He moved his lips with mine and my arms wrapped around his neck.

Six days ago, I was just a girl looking to find freedom, some fun, but most importantly to figure out some kind of plan for my life. My entire existence revolved around hiding. Afraid to look over my shoulder. I'd hoped one day to be able to live in the moment, unafraid, and to live a peaceful ever after. And there I was on a ship, nearly killed like my classmates, but for the first time, I felt alive, free and safe.

After the shower, we dressed in dry clothes, like we'd changed in front of each other a thousand times before. Then we laid down and I nestled myself in the crook of his arm against my pillow. I don't think either of us had spoken a word since before the shower, but what had been a comfortable silence was starting to linger too long.

"What are you thinking about?" I asked.

A little more silence followed, and I wondered if he was sleeping, but he shifted slightly, pulling me a little closer.

"I'm just thinking about tomorrow."

"What about it?"

He waited a moment. "I don't want it to come."

"Me either," I murmured.

"But it is," he said.

"I know, so what do we do?"

"Whatever you want," he whispered.

"I want to be able to stay together."

"You know that's not possible," he said in the same calm tone.

I took a deep breath. "We can make something work."

I waited for him to reply, wondering if he was going to pull away and list reasons why it was impossible, but he didn't.

"I'm willing if you are," he murmured.

I sat up on one elbow. "I am." Even if we couldn't see each other. I wanted him to know I was getting serious. "I don't care how crazy it is. I want to stay in touch. We can start there."

He lifted onto one elbow too and gave me a kiss. "We can start there," he said, before laying back down.

I lowered myself onto his arm. "You aren't just telling me what I want to hear are you?"

"No. I've thought about coming up with every reason to avoid disappointment from it not working out but the truth is, I don't want to. I'm just going to take it day by day. Whatever you want, I'll go with for as long as you want."

"What I want?"

"Yes. Because I want you. It's that simple."

His words shocked me. I couldn't have planned it any other way, and the impossibility of them didn't even matter to me. I wrapped my arms around him and nestled my leg between his like he was a body pillow.

After a few moments of silence, I started to think more practically. "How can I reach you? You don't have a phone."

"I have email, and there are ways I can call you if you want."

Of course I wanted that. It was sounding promising and on the side of normal. We lay there for a little while longer and then he told me he felt it was almost time for him to go. I don't think I truly grasped what he meant exactly. My eyes just became heavy and my thoughts became distant sounds inside my own mind.

I wanted to find out more details. To make more plans before tomorrow, but my body felt incredibly light and the space around me became too cozy to even question the sleepiness. Soon I heard myself mumble some lazy slurs about goodnight and I drifted off to a deep sleep that came unnaturally fast.

J. P.

Chapter 28

It took a lot of effort to stay awake longer than her. My mind usually grew heavy but I fought it hard. I never knew exactly what happened when I left one place for another. The last thing I remembered each time was extreme fatigue and then loss of consciousness. It was a feeling coming on then, which made me realize it was almost time. I didn't want to leave her, but tomorrow we would have had no choice.

I meant what I said about trying whatever she wanted afterward. But having a dramatic goodbye in broad daylight was not how I wanted to remember her. I only hoped she'd understand.

The more I thought about nowhere to go, the more sleepy she became. It was like a drug, heavy in the air, and the more I thought about it, the more right it felt to let it happen. So when she fell asleep first, I slid out of bed long enough to write her a note and then lay back beside her. I took in how her body felt against mine. How her hair smelled and how good life felt next to her. And then I kissed her cheek and let myself fall asleep, not knowing if I'd wake up somewhere else or not.

When sunrise came, I was lying on a lounge chair on some unknown upper deck. It was a different ship, in a different place, but the familiar sunrise was there. I'd seen it many times from many different angles. Looking at it now was somehow less disappointing than every other morning. Even though I had no idea where I was, there was a feeling of a new type of longing for the first time. I had no socks and no shoes and my day would start like every other time. Finding necessities, hopefully a room this time, along with an identity. But this time, I had something to look forward to.

Avery

Chapter 29

When I woke up, I had no idea what time it was. J.P. was no longer next to me and I assumed he must have gone to the bathroom. I reached over and grabbed my phone, squinted and glanced at the screen. It was 7 a.m. I rolled back over, snuggling my face back into the soft pillow. After a few, long moments, I sat up looking. The only light was from the hall under the doorway, but my eyes had adjusted enough to see the room was empty. I sat up a little more and turned on the light. J.P. was nowhere in sight, but the cabin door was bolted from the inside.

I walked over to the empty bathroom and that's when it struck me. On the nightstand was a piece of paper with a pen lying beside it. My heart sank as I picked up the note.

It read:

Dear Avery,

I'm sorry to leave like this, but it's time. I meant what I said. I'm willing for as long as you are.

J.P.

He also added his email address.

I don't know how long I sat there just watching and waiting and rereading the note several times. And the longer I sat there, the longer I felt that he was gone.

Shortly after 8 a.m, Rebecca had texted me. The ship was heading back to shore and we would be there by late afternoon. She told me the coast guard had been called in to look for both Mr. Wells and Kate Thompson. Packing and preparing to go home was surreal. I felt like a zombie preparing to walk off the ship.

By the time I'd gotten to the lobby, Rebecca had caught up with me. "Where is he?" she asked.

I looked down and shrugged.

"Is he here?" she pressed.

I shook my head. "I don't think so."

"So he's gone?"

"Pretty sure he is. He just left me this."

I handed her the note and she read it.

"Okay, so you have his email. That's good." She gave it back to me and smiled and carried on like nothing was wrong. It was just another way she knew how to make me feel like everything was good.

When we got to the terminal, my mom and sister were waiting. My mom gave me a huge hug that spoke all of her worries and all of her relief at the same time. It felt good to be on solid ground too, but part of me was longing already. I turned around and caught sight of the ginormous cruise ship, just wondering where J.P. was. Where he had been and where he would be going. The ship was set against an endless backdrop of ocean. He could have been anywhere. A hollow feeling in my chest struck me, and I took a deep breath trying to push it back in my mind.

The following week, Rebecca and I attended Erick's funeral. I don't think there is ever a sadness quite like losing a kid. His uncle spoke about another place where Erick could be happy. It sounded good, but it was just a hope. They never found Kate Thompson or Mr. Wells, and after two weeks, we attended Kate's funeral too. It rained so bad that day. Like a horrible storm that never ended for her. I felt terrible knowing she went into the water just like me. I knew J.P. had done everything he could to save her too, but it didn't make her loss resonate any less.

My life was so out of sorts. All I could think about was Kate Thompson and Mr. Wells at school. The only time I felt at peace was when I tried to push thoughts of J.P. in there, but all that did was take me back to the ship and all the things I couldn't fix about it. I had emailed him the day I got back and we spoke every day, but I was losing hope.

He was making every attempt to keep my spirits up, but I was going through a period of what next. I wanted to help him, but I was a mess thinking about death all the time. The anxiety of just living without any forward progress made me depressed. Even Rebecca became worried about me.

Then after about a month, J.P. stopped calling and replying to my emails, making me more paranoid that I'd pushed him away. There had been no explanation. No reason. Nothing. He just stopped responding and that led me from feeling helpless to confused. I stayed up late, night after night, emotions shifting from worry, to anger, to sadness. And the cycle starting all over again.

Then graduation came and he still didn't answer my emails. It was completely depressing. But being the friend that Rebecca always was, she went out of her way to cheer me up. She surprised me with a trip to New York for us with some money she had saved up.

It was a super nice gesture, but I hadn't been interested in any more trips. It wasn't until she said Staten Island with a super excited look on her face that I perked up.

She had been doing research on the *Titanic* every chance she had once we got home. After a while, I started to ignore her and let her do what she does, which is look up and obsess about all kinds of stories. But I remembered her talking about Staten Island as being one of the largest Italian populations in New York. This was after she said she believed the woman J.P. saved was Italian and probably settled there.

"What are you up to?" I asked, feeling an odd sense of hope and apprehension at once.

"You know I have my ways."

"Yes, but what's going on?"

"Ok fine. I'll spill."

I had been interested in her research, but never got my hopes up about anything in particular. But, after she had my undivided attention, she spilled everything she'd found out. According to her research, there was a living relative of the woman J.P. had saved. She was convinced that a blood relative could break the curse, and she found one living on Staten Island. It was a crazy idea, but I was starting to think that nothing was impossible.

We left super early on a Saturday morning, so we would have all day to find this relative. I was terrified to go for fear of the unknown, the known, and all of the in-between. But we went. Rebecca looked completely relaxed, the whole way. She kept herself busy on the train by reading a book she'd found about curses. It was as if she knew talking to me about things, would make me even more on edge.

I kept thinking about J.P. being out there some-where all alone. Or maybe he wasn't. Maybe he'd moved on and found someone else. I went round and round, but if I believed anything he'd told me, that wasn't possible. He was out there and he was avoiding real contact for some reason.

After the train, we took a bus to a stop that took us close enough to walk to a trendy neighborhood packed with small apartments. The address was tucked away in a charming courtyard that was overgrown with every color of flowers possible. Rebecca led the way to the door and I hung back unable to stop thinking about the fact that just maybe, just maybe, we could actually break J.P.'s curse.

The small woman who answered was tan, completely grayed and moved slowly, but she had a confidence about her. My mind was lost in past and present and my heart was beating at the enormity of the aura, but the air felt peaceful at the same time.

I don't know what I would have done without Rebecca because she took charge of everything. The woman was reluctant to let us in, but somehow Rebecca put her at ease. We were seated on a small floral sofa covered in multicolored knitted afghans. Rebecca started with our story right away. She told the woman everything that happened and exactly what J.P. had told me. After staring at us wide-eyed for a long time, the woman looked down and told us that the little child who J.P. helped save was her mother. And not only that, her grandmother had kept a diary telling all about the boy who saved them. The woman went into a small doorway off the family room and was gone for several minutes.

"This is crazy exciting," Rebecca whispered. I was too frozen to speak. "This could actually work," she urged. After a minute, she nudged my elbow. "Don't you think?"

"I don't know," was all I could say through my raspy throat.

The woman returned several moments later with photos and stories of her family's survival.

Once she was done, Rebecca scooted a little closer to the edge of the sofa.

"Do you think you can break the curse?" she asked, hopeful.

I watched as the soft smile quickly faded and she closed the book. The woman was seventy-eight now and made it very clear she wanted nothing to do with the curse. She'd had nightmares over the years that were haunting her about the boy lost in the water. The last thing she wanted to do was revisit the curse.

Rebecca scooted closer so her knee was touching the woman. "But don't you think that means you should break the curse? And maybe the nightmares will stop?"

The woman stood, still clutching the album, and opened the front door. "The curse will cease when you stop believing in it."

"What's that supposed to mean?" Rebecca asked, not moving.

"You go and have a good day," she replied pointing outside and standing a little taller.

"But–"

At that point a younger woman appeared from a back hallway which seemed to give the surviving granddaughter more urgency.

"I said there will be no attempts at magic here. Goodbye."

She sent us away completely defeated. We had stood in the courtyard for several minutes gathering our wits and figuring out our next move. We were just about to leave when a girl about our age came running out from a narrow walkway on the side of the house.

The girl looked down, her dark hair falling over her eyes. "I heard what you told my Nonna."

"You did?" Rebecca asked, stepping in eagerly.

Our gazes fell to what appeared to be an old leather book, tattered and worn, pressed tightly against her chest. "I can help you," she said.

"Really?" I asked, shocked.

"Yes. It's something my great grandmother wrote about in here. She wondered about that boy for a long time."

"She did?" I looked at Rebecca standing with a hopeful smile.

"Yeah," the girl continued. "My mom goes to work at six o'clock and my Nonna will be cooking dinner. Come around back then."

Our mouths were agape as she walked away nervously scanning her surroundings.

"OMG," Rebecca said. "What just happened?"

"I have no idea."

"Did you see that book?"

I nodded, still trying to replay the event.

"I want to see that book," she said.

"So what do we do?"

She looped her arm through mine. "We go kill some time."

We left and grabbed a bite to eat at a coffee shop and replayed the strange turn of events over half sandwiches and pastries. Rebecca was more than excited. "I wish I could read that whole book," she mused. "I bet it has so many cool things in it. Did you see how old it looked?"

"Yeah. But I'd settle for the cliff notes."

"What? You would say such a thing. You can't rush stuff like this. Let me do the talking."

And that, I wasn't going to argue with. We finished up and went back when she had told us to, and it was a moment we will never forget. The girl met us at the door and took us straight up to her room. It was small, but cozy and neatly decorated with dozens of dream-catchers that made it look like a cool getaway.

"So this is my room," she said avoiding our gazes sheepishly.

"It's nice," Rebecca responded kindly.

The girl looked up at Rebecca and relaxed her shoulders a little. "My name is Mia."

"Nice to meet you. I'm Rebecca and this is my friend Avery."

I gave a small wave, "Hi."

"So, how do you guys know about the curse?"

Rebecca pointed her thumb in my direction. "She knows the guy that was cursed. She's trying to help him."

"Wow," she breathed, sitting on the edge of her bed, clutching a book to her chest. "So it is real."

"Appears so," Rebecca said.

Mia stared at the floor for a long moment. "I'd heard bits and pieces over the years. Sometimes my mom and Nonna would argue about bad dreams and say it had something to do with the curse. A strange sadness has hung over our family, and it wasn't just because of the people who hadn't survived. It's because of that unresolved curse, and I want to help, because it's worth a try. And then, maybe my family can move on."

"So you'll help us?" Rebecca asked.

"I'll help you," she said. "I don't want anyone else to suffer."

We had no idea if it would work, but she admitted that she'd had the same dreams about a boy that her grandmother had all her life. Based on that and the fact that she was a blood relative, we hoped she could also break it. I had a shirt that J.P. had worn and Rebecca had his picture from the book. There were two items Rebecca thought we needed, based on all of her research about curses.

With both items in her hand, the girl repeated the words her great-grandmother spoke many years ago and said it shall be no more. Joseph Percy Carter shall no longer be confined.

I'd like to say that there was some flickering lights' moment, or some earth-shaking, but there wasn't. The only thing that I did feel was a small sense of peace and warmth at the moment she was finished. And for some reason, I just felt that maybe it had worked. She and Rebecca were more confident than me. They even exchanged numbers to keep in touch, and she let Rebecca skim through the old book.

When Rebecca and I got home, the first thing I did was think about emailing him but I didn't know what to say. I didn't know where he was, what he was thinking or who he was with.

I decided that it wasn't about me and him. It was really about setting him free and for him to be happy. More than anything else.

And so I sat down and typed.

J.P.,

I have no idea why you stopped responding to me. I've been angry, mad, confused and sad all at once. But I've decided that it's not really about me anymore. It's about you, so I hope you get this.

Rebecca found the granddaughter of the woman you saved that night. We think we were able to get your curse removed. I want you to know I've never met anyone who makes me feel like you do, and I really want to see you again. Next Saturday, the *Pristine* will be docking and I will be there if you decide to come. Even if you don't and you find that your curse is really lifted now, please write me back so I know that you are free.

Avery

J. P.

Chapter 30

I had called, or emailed Avery almost everyday after she got home. She became pretty much the only thing I looked forward to everyday. It was the first time I cared about someone from a distance. All I thought about was her safety, or happiness, or sadness. I had an admitted obsession to know more about her, to feel close to her.

One afternoon, I was on the computer and something made me start searching for information about her past, to really know who she was. Or maybe it was something else. I don't know, but I found myself researching the name she told me was her real one. Surprisingly, a new article came right up with a headline that made me want to close the page, but it was too late.

Words stared back at me like, "killed," and "double murder." My gaze continued over the phrase, *The man was killed along side his sixteen-year-old daughter, Johanna Roberts, at his downtown office.*

No. I tried to quickly convince myself that I'd heard her name wrong, or that she'd lied to me. Determined, I kept searching. Over and over, article after article all dated just a year ago, said the same thing. But it was the last article that made me back away from the computer.

It was a perfectly clear picture of Avery and her father standing together, smiling. The Avery I had wanted to be mine. Right at the center of another article describing their double murder. I put my face in my hands. I remembered her smile, her laughter, her anger, her passion for life and me. There was nothing lifeless about it. She was real, as real as me. My mind raced, trying to understand. She couldn't have been killed. That was impossible. But everything was impossible. Including me. I came to the most unsettling realization and typed in Joseph Percy Carter and leaned forward.

I was instantly met with the same passenger manifests and stories of my perished family. A few articles on missing bodies. I sat back in my chair, staring at the screen. After a few minutes, I leaned forward again and searched my father's name. There was an instant result of an article about his net worth at the time of the sinking. It seemed like something I already knew, but I was grasping at straws, so I leaned in and kept reading. It wasn't until I got toward the bottom, that the discrepancy stood out.

The article said that his entire fortune went to my uncle. His brother was the only living heir and he received his family inheritance. I sat back knowing that this didn't seem right. This is not how I remembered it. I specifically remember my mom's brother getting the inheritance. He set up bank accounts for me.

I swallowed and tapped back into the searching. Information on my mother's brother was much harder to find, but when I did find it, my stomach dropped. He had passed away just a couple of months after the sinking in a tractor accident on his Pennsylvania farm. Never a rich, wealthy man, and I started to remember him that way. Just like the words said. My mind felt heavy. My body felt tense.

I exited out of the pages and went back to my room. I lay on my bed staring at the ceiling for several more hours, wondering if any of my memories were even real. Why would I think the wrong uncle got the inheritance? Was my memory a fabrication? Was anything real? That's when I began to fear that maybe I never actually survived. And what did that mean for me? What did that mean for Avery? It was a truth I'd be able to handle for myself, but not for her. That's the day I stopped calling and answering her emails. How could I tell her any of it?

She had emailed me every day for weeks and with each one, the tone got more and more angry. Her temper didn't make forgetting her any easier. I pictured her cornering me in her room and letting me have it. It was even a moment like that, that made me miss her more.

My mind became a constant prison, not knowing who I was, where I was, or where she was and what all of it meant. I even began to wonder if she was a fabrication. I had just started to get back to a somewhat normal routine when I ended up back on the *Pristine*. And of all places, it was on a couch inside the Tiki bar. It was an instant flashback of her standing by the railing, with Scumbag behind her, looking completely terrified. I attempted to blink away the memories, but all the concern I'd felt that night for her came rushing back.

I'd worked for years and years to make each day tolerable, only for it to all come crashing down after one day. I wanted the memories of her to be over, thinking maybe I could rewind time for both of us.

There was no map for how to handle such a thing, so I found myself in the media center. I believed that if I could end things with her the right way, then maybe we could pretend we never met at all.

I went to my email and saw only one unread message within the last three weeks. Her email address stared back at me. It had been 4 days since she sent the email and it felt like I'd stared at it just as long before opening it.

I expected her to let me have it for abandoning her yet again, but her soft tone stood out to me first. Then it was words like save, curse, removed, free. I read them a dozen times and they never changed. Stumped, I closed out the page and turned completely around. It was insanity. Or maybe it was some cruel trick to give me hope.

Or maybe it was my own mind messing with me to lure me back into some twisted reality. That is exactly what it was. I'd convinced myself that I needed to cut ties with the idea of Avery more than ever. Otherwise I'd go insane.

I closed the email and I went straight to the café in search of something to help me clear my head. I sat down with a drink and full plate of food and looked around for someone to help me forget. There were a lot of girls, but one stood out the most. Confident. Shoulders back, not a hair out of place, looking for attention. And she looked nothing like Avery.

She saw me watching her, so I gave her an easy grin and looked away. After a few casual moments, I glanced back and she was still watching me.

I took a last bite of toast and carried a drink out to the deck. Within minutes, her shoulder length black hair blew in the breeze to my left. Side by side, we watched the ocean for several long moments. Things felt normal again, if it ever was, or could be.

"It's a nice view," I said, convincing myself that I could have whatever reality I wanted.

"Yeah, it is. Really pretty." Her voice was higher pitched than I expected, but that wasn't a bad thing, I told myself.

"My name is John," I said, looking at the view to the right. I'd used the fake name a thousand times, but using it again was a disappointment that I blinked away.

"Hi John. I'm Savannah."

"It's a nice name."

She moved her hair out of her face and I couldn't help but notice that she didn't move it because it was in her way. She wanted the strands to be exactly where they were supposed to be. It was a direct contrast to Avery who always had flyaways. And yet, no matter how out of place, they looked perfect on her. "Thanks. Where are you from?" she said.

I forced away thoughts of the very person I wasn't doing a good job of forgetting. Obviously. "New York," I said. It was the truth, and it still felt like a disappointment saying it to her.

"Me too. That's pretty amazing."

She shifted closer so her shoulder touched mine and smiled again. I turned in response and she inched in. Her chest was almost against mine and would have been if I breathed too heavy. I stayed steady, watching her.

When she leaned in a little, the hairs on the back of my neck stood. A pretty girl was in my personal space, giving me every signal in the book and I felt like a complete idiot.

"I'm sorry," I said. "I have somewhere to be."

Her lips turned into a pout. "Why? Do you have a girlfriend or something?"

I looked at her, seeing Avery's face come and go. "Something like that."

"That's a shame," she said.

"I'm sorry," I told her again, before walking away. I wasn't sorry about Avery. I was simply sorry that I'd wasted a complete stranger's time. I shook my head and took myself back to my room feeling like a jerk. I showered. I changed clothes, but everything I did led back to memories of Avery. There I was alone, and after two attempts at leaving her hanging, she was dangling kindness and the temptation of a relationship over my head in the midst of my confusion.

I lay down and stared at the ceiling. Safe, curse, remove, free. Impossible. I tried several times to get to port in the years after the sinking. More times than I can count, and each time, drowsiness, leading to unconsciousness, leading to the next place to nowhere. Meeting Avery had made me start hoping for the chance again, but then I found the articles. And now, with the opportunity dangling over my head, I didn't know what to believe anymore.

I closed my eyes to shake those memories and what I saw behind them was a cross between a dream and a vivid nightmare. I saw my own hand push up pink fabric from a small body, a child maybe. It was so cold and hot at the same time. Panic in my chest burned as I felt my body assaulted by frozen pins and needles. There was nowhere to go to escape the black, icy water and suddenly the cold pierced my hot lungs, flooding them with pain. Every kind of pain I could think of, and it only ended when I woke up on a new ship. It was like every other time, but there was one detail that stood out this time. The name of the ship was the *Californian.* I blinked away the vision and jerked upright in the bed. I was sweating.

In all the years I could remember, I had never had a single dream, so whatever that was shook me hard. The air felt dry, and suffocating. It was a moment where loneliness made me reflect on my state of mind. What had I gotten myself into with just one encounter with a girl on a cruise?

I lay back down, unsettled. The dream almost replicated the many times I had sunk to the bottom of the ocean, hoping to put an end to whatever state I had been in all these years. But each time, I'd woken up elsewhere, and each time I'd wanted not to wake up. It was mentally traumatizing to go through drowning over and over. But in this memory, or dream, or nightmare, whatever it was, there was never a moment where I gave in to the water. I had been fighting it the entire time, panicked and in pain, until there was no more pain and, miraculously, I was on a new ship. A ship full of corpses. All dead except me.

I had ignored that detail for many years, because afterwards, I had learned that there were no survivors picked up by the *Californian*. Only corpses, and there it was. What I'd refused to see, all this time. Time that suddenly came down to this moment.

In the morning, I was still in the same room, and there was a piece of paper on the floor near the door. I walked over and picked it up, my hand having a hard time holding it still. It was a settlement sheet. I'd never gotten close enough to shore to get one of these, and there I was looking at a statement made out to John Smith. Balance of zero. Whatever state, or place I was in, was crashing in on me and the reality was going to come out one way or another.

I walked over to the trash and dropped it in there, watching it sway its way down to the bottom of the can. Despite what was staring me in the face, there still seemed no way, after all these years, that I would be able to walk off of this ship.

Now, all of a sudden, all the questions hit me hard. Did I want to be free of this? What does this mean? I'd wanted it for so long, but now that it could possibly be, did I *really* want it?

I sat there staring at the wall, trying to figure out what was actually going to happen. It was just impossible, so I prepared for the fatigue, and the unconsciousness and closed my eyes. Minutes ticked by. Then more minutes. Eventually, an aggressive knock at my door brought me back to my surroundings.

I looked through the peephole to see a crew member standing there reading a chart, while tapping a foot. I opened the door to orders that it was time to leave. All passengers, including me, needed to vacate their rooms. We could use the common and lounge areas until our group was called for debarkation. He gave more instructions, but I tuned them out after hearing the word, "debarkation." Not a word seemed real. I didn't even know if *I* was real at that point.

After packing my stuff in my backpack, I went over to the cafe, unsure of what to do with myself. Almost feeling ill at the sight of food, I left there just as quickly.

I found myself maneuvering around travelers who rolled suitcases between crew members, who were directing passengers. It was organized chaos. My heart beats pounded, my palms were getting sweaty.

I went up to one of the upper decks to find a good seat to just look out over the ocean for a sense of normalcy again. It was the first time I actually wanted to fall asleep and escape to somewhere else. Anxiety was making me question the idea of actually walking off of a ship, and into the unknown.

I spent time looking out over the water, but my gaze was drawn toward the shore where I could actually see people at the port. Cars I had never seen in person. It was surreal. But it was there, right in front of my eyes.

I took a deep breath and turned myself toward the signs and pointing crew members. As I neared the exit area, there were people ahead of me and behind that left no room for indecision. I did everything to take slow, steady breaths without slowing up the process for everyone else.

When it was my turn, I took the first step over the ship threshold and the bottom of my shoe hit the walkway. It felt like the world was spinning, but I put one foot in front of the other and walked with nothing less than muscle memory. There were about a million different thoughts clouding my mind, but I kept walking, slowly, but steadily.

I put my sweaty hands in my pockets as each passenger in front of me showed their cruise pass. When the attendant saw me, she quickly glanced at me and said, "Have a nice day." Without a blink, she then reached for the pass of the person behind me. I paused a moment, thinking it was too easy, but the person behind me was moving into my space. It was a feeling of freedom like nothing I could describe. All the years of virtually free travel, free food and clothing, none of it had felt as it did at that moment.

I walked along the port, leaving space between me and the ship walls. A salty breeze was behind me, but in front of me was city air. Musty and humid and I recognized it instantly, even after all these years.

I kept walking, taking in a long breath as my senses adjusted to the new surroundings. And then I realized, I had no direction. On a ship, you can keep walking in circles and never end up needing to make a real decision. Somewhere and nowhere was a circular rotation on a ship. You would always end up back at the beginning at some point. This was a somewhere and nowhere without an ending. It was the worst kind of nowhere and suddenly I stopped, standing with my hands in my pockets and looked around at all the people who had purpose.

To my right were earthy green and yellow pleather waiting chairs in rows along the windows. I blinked away the sixties era, still unsure if I was in a dream. Time caught back up at the sight of several people sitting in them, staring at their phones. The time contrast didn't give me enough reason to relax, and I was starting to second guess being there.

When a small crowd parted in front of me, I saw Avery standing, looking around, gaze roaming from left to right, and back again. Her natural beauty struck me just as I remembered even though she looked tired and anxious. She paused a long moment at the sight of me and then squeezed through the crowd, straight toward me.

Without another pause, she wrapped her arms around my neck and my face fell, buried in her hair. I don't think I moved, didn't even take my hands out of my pockets. I just let her hug me, for a very long time without speaking.

I realized then, standing there, that every ounce of apprehension, every ounce of nervousness, every foreign feeling was gone. I slid my hands from my pockets and put my arms around her too. And even if it were only for a little while, I could pretend that everything was how it should be.

Avery

Chapter 31

I had watched passengers disembark for over an hour, but was determined to stay until the very last person. And then I spotted him. He looked tired and almost like he wanted to head back toward the dock. But he was there. I couldn't believe it. He'd gotten my message and could have tried to go anywhere, and he came here. It was the only answer I needed. I moved so fast, forgetting everything about the last few weeks. I wrapped my arms around his chest with urgent force, but he stood firm, letting me hold him.

"It worked," I finally breathed.

He continued to hold me. "It worked."

"I can't believe it."

"Me neither."

It was then when I pulled back to see his face to make sure it was real. His dark gaze was heavy, but gave me no indication of how he felt. His jaw was tense, as if he wanted to say something, but remained silent. So silent that it seemed to overpower the loud and crowded terminal. It occurred to me that he was completely out of his comfort zone and this was no place for us to talk.

I took my arm and looped it through his, taking his hand with my other hand. "Come on, let's go."

It felt completely warm and a soothing feeling I tried not to get carried away with, crept up my arm. We walked toward my car while he just looked around, taking everything in. "I want to show you something," I said.

I didn't know if being around a ton of people in a new city would make him anxious, so I drove him somewhere I thought he would like. The route had everything, from crowded street corners, traffic, new buildings, old buildings, and even tree-lines and waterviews. I expected to hear a lot of wows, or for him to have a look of awe or curiosity at the very least. But he was mellow. Too mellow.

"Everything okay?"

He looked over at me and gave a lazy smile. "I'm just taking it all in."

"I guess this is pretty new for you."

He didn't respond and it was making me nervous, but we'd reached the parking area of a nice park in Upper Manhattan.

We walked up several paths that meandered through a perfect spring backdrop. We sat down once we found a private bench with a great view of the city and water.

I didn't want to insult him by acting like he was from another planet, but I had so many questions. How he felt, what he thought. But coming to the top of all the questions was just the simple fact that he may not be here to see me.

"Good to know you were getting my messages," I said. He looked away from the view and down at his lap. "A simple reply would have been nice." He began to crack his knuckles which was the first time I'd seen him do that.

I wished I hadn't griped as soon as the words came out of my mouth. He shook his head ever so slightly which I picked up on but decided to let my irritation fizzle out some. I missed him unhealthily and was more glad to be sitting beside him than words could measure. But my feelings were my feelings and he owed me, at least, some sort of explanation.

"I deserve everything you have to say about me," he said.

That was a start, but I didn't know what to think. "In all fairness, that will depend on what you have to say about yourself first."

He went back to watching the water. "What do you mean?"

"What do I mean? Why the change? Why did you stop answering me?"

His gaze shifted to some chirping blue birds nearby, and he took a deep breath. I'd seen him conflicted a few times before, but never like this. I would've thought he'd have been ecstatic by now. "What's wrong J.P.? You're worrying me."

After a moment he turned my way. "Avery, what if meeting me changed your entire life for the worst? Everything you knew or thought about yourself was wrong. Would you have still wanted to meet me?"

I wasn't expecting him to go that deep, but I thought for a moment. "Well," I said shrugging, "my life did change when I met you. And I liked it."

I thought I saw a slight smile forming, but then it went away. "No," he said. "I mean, everything you thought you knew about yourself. What if you weren't who you thought you were?"

"What are you talking about?"

He shook his head and stood. "I don't think I can do this."

"Wait," I was beyond confused. "So are you walking away? Again? You can't be serious?"

He sighed and threw his hands up and grabbed his backpack. "I never asked for this."

"Asked for what?"

"For any of this!" He stood up and started walking towards the path.

"Well I did!" I called, stopping him in his tracks. "So there. I asked for this. Even if you don't care."

He turned back. "I do care. What did you mean that you asked for this?"

Everything with him felt like decisions needed to be made now or never. It was the pressure or the thought of him disappearing at sea or somewhere that made me want to leave with no regrets. So I spoke the truth.

"I asked for someone like you. Someone who I can be with that makes me feel like you do. Most of the time."

He just stood there and waited, so I sat back down. "If it makes you so miserable, then go ahead. Go."

I crossed my arms and legs completely frustrated.

After a moment, I felt him come close and sit back down next to me, making me feel uncomfortable and vulnerable. "When did you ask that?" he murmured.

I let out a deep breath. "I don't know. Like ever since I was little I guess. Just wanted to find the right guy and live happily ever after. Who knew it would be with someone so unstable."

He ignored my insult and my pout. "It all makes sense. Avery, I stopped calling because I found something out that I thought would hurt you."

"Like what?"

"I mean really, really hurt you. It will make you wish you never met me, if I tell you."

"That's not possible. The only thing that can hurt me is lies. Just tell me."

He rubbed his forehead and dropped his backpack. A young couple walked by with a curious chocolate lab and he waited until we were alone again. "You told me about your father."

My body froze, knowing I didn't want to go there. "He's off limits."

"I don't want to talk about what happened to him."

"Good, because neither do I."

"I want to talk about what happened to you."

"I told you. I went to work with him and I saw him get killed. Then I testified and that's it."

"What happened after you saw him killed?"

"I don't want to talk about it."

He put his hand on my leg. "Please, it's important."

"Why?

"Because it is."

I thought back, pushing out any possible image of blood. "I don't remember."

"Think. Did you call someone there? Did you leave?"

I started to feel my heartbeat in my chest. "I don't know."

"Think for me. It's very important if you want to know the truth."

"I told you, I don't know."

"Think," he urged.

I wanted to push him away, literally. This wasn't about me. And he was making it like it was.

"Why are you asking me to remember? What's wrong with you?"

"It's just important. Please. Try to remember."

"I don't want to."

"Please, just try."

I was fuming so hard, I had to look away. I wiped my eyes to stop the tears and took slow, deep breaths. If he wanted to know, then fine. I closed my eyes, remembering screaming as I heard the gun shots.

Why did I scream? He told me not to. But I did. I saw those men shoot him as I watched through the crack in the bathroom door. My father fell with a thud and I screamed. He pointed toward me and croaked the words, "Go." That's when the dark haired man hovered over him and sliced his throat. I screamed again. I was just a kid.

I felt the tears fall down my face then and I felt them again as I was remembering. I cried over his chest and when I turned around there was a police officer in the corner. An instant sense of comfort that everything would be alright came over me. I ran toward him, knowing I wouldn't dare forget a single detail about my father's murderers.

The only thing I'd wanted since that day was for those guys to go to jail and for my mom and sister to be ok, which was all happening. I'd also wanted for me to have a normal life when I grew up. With someone to be with that made me feel happy. And I thought I had it, no matter how crazy it seemed. It was worth every minute of it. But now, J.P. wanted me to remember the worst day of my life.

I turned around with tears in my eyes. "So there you have it. The police came. That was it."

"Do you remember testifying?"

"Yeah." A blank cloud formed behind my eyes as I tried to recap what happened. "I think so."

"So you don't actually remember testifying?"

"It's hard to remember ok? I don't want to remember."

"I know it's hard. But it's important. Try to think. What happened after you saw the officer Avery? What next?"

"Oh my gosh." The tears were just dripping one by one. I turned away, so angry.

The feeling of anger assaulted my memory. The officer looked angry too and I focused on his face. That's when I felt someone snatch me by my hair and lift me off the ground. I screamed again, shocked and not understanding. A cold, hard object pressed against my throat and a sharp pain dulled under a warm drip down my neck. As my vision blurred, the officer walked toward me and watched me fall. It was the craziest thing to see him standing with his hands in his pockets.

"Oh my gosh," I repeated turning back around. J.P. put both hands on my leg, but I swatted him away. He continued on and grabbed me, pressing my face between his palms. I shook my head pushing out the confusion. Why was he doing this to me?

He'd stolen my father's shirt and caused me fury then and he was doing it again. Why had I let him in? "I don't understand why you are doing this?" I mumbled as he pulled me into his shirt. I tried to push away again, but he held me still.

"I'm sorry Avery. I just wanted to know more about you. And I found it online."

I pushed away enough to look at him. "Found what online?"

"I won't tell you. If you can't remember, I won't tell you."

"Don't you understand? I don't know what happened. Even if I remembered more, I don't know what happened. Just tell me."

And just like that, he was conflicted again. He closed his dark eyes and opened them in slow motion.

"Say it!"

His eyes were moist causing a glassy reflection where I could almost see myself. And then he spoke. "The article said you died too. I'm so sorry."

"No, I was ten years old J.P. You're making me remember something that's not possible."

"You weren't ten Avery."

"What?"

"Think. It was just last year."

"I'm so over this." I shook my head quickly and walked past him. I heard no footsteps following and I didn't care. It was just too much. Maybe the article was protecting our identities. There could be so many reasons it was incorrect, but him forcing that day back on me was something I couldn't get past. And just when I thought I was far enough away to leave him and the nightmare behind me, he called out.

"I don't think I survived the sinking."

My breath paused, and I turned around. "What did you say?"

"It's not just you. I think both of us died."

I shortened the distance between us. "Are you crazy?"

"I could be, but it doesn't change what I think."

"Why are you making this up? I have a mom, a sister, friends."

"Do you?"

"Yes, and they're real."

"Real how?"

"Real!"

He may not have had any close relatives anymore, but I did and they were waiting for me to come home. And there I was standing with him, doubting everything about what I thought was real. He may very well have been uniquely special, but he was real too.

"Listen to me." He grabbed my hands and put them over his chest. "I don't think I'm alive."

"Why do you keep saying that?"

"Because. I've lived a hundred years and it feels like 10. I've never had to want for anything other than what I thought was freedom. But I realized that's not what I wanted at all. I wanted you. All these years, I wanted you. And then you came. I didn't realize that was the key until you just told me that you wished for me. You've gotten everything you've wanted. What if it's not physically us. What if this is us after we've died? In some perfect world."

I wanted to be sick. I needed to sit down. "What if our minds," he continued, "are what carried on in years, like souls, and we have created the life we want."

I shook my head, going back to everything real I'd ever known before meeting him. My mom and my sister. They were real and happy. Always happy. My mom was protective, but happy. The more I thought about it, the more I'd never seen my mom sad. I even tried to think back to after my father's murder and she wasn't sad. She smiled, always. She was even so proud when I testified and put them away. But not a single tear. Why?

My friend Rebecca. She was exactly what I would ask for in a friend. Strong, smart, sweet, funny, trustworthy, loyal. She was everything perfect and true. And she never got sad either.

The only time I could think about any struggle or obstacle was on the ship. The ship that led me to J.P. Why would that be?

"I don't understand."

"I don't either."

"But you're the one saying it."

"I wasn't going to say anything, because I knew it would hurt you. That's why I cut things off. I thought you'd be better off going back to the way things were. I'm sorry."

"You're sorry?"

"Yes, I am. But, I just can't take back what I saw. Once I was with you, I couldn't keep it from you."

We sat there in complete silence for many long moments. I made a point of listening to the sounds of trees moving and birds chirping, and then he started speaking.

"After I read about you, I looked up my family too. My maternal uncle never could have given me any of my inheritance, because he never got it. It was all in my head. I think that's what my mind thought should happen to help myself, and so it happened."

"Are you telling me you made it all up and it happened?"

He nodded. "My uncle was a poor farmer. I wanted him to inherit it I guess."

"You're serious? Or is this a test, or something I'm failing?"

"No Avery. Maybe. I don't know. Maybe we're both failing it. But, it makes more sense to me than a curse. Maybe it's an afterlife. Just a place where we could carry on, how we would want to."

"How we want to? Just make it up?"

"That's what I think."

"So my mom, sister?"

"They are how you want them to be."

"Happy?"

"If that's how you want them to be."

"They would want me to be happy."

"And you probably have been. Until you met me."

I instinctively shook my head. "No, I'm happy because of you."

"I feel the same."

He said it so easily.

"What about Mr. Wells, Kate and Erick? Why would people die in our minds. That's cruel."

"I thought about that too, and we never saw any bodies. Maybe we both needed something traumatic to pull us together. Otherwise we'd still be wandering around aimlessly."

"This is insane. I'm trying, but I can't believe any of this."

"You saw what happened to you Avery."

"I'm not dead."

"Then don't be."

I shook my head blinking a dozen times. "What does that even mean?"

"Just be who you want to be, I guess."

"What if I choose to go back home?"

"Then go back home."

"And forget about everything you told me?"

"If that's what you want to do."

"What about you?"

He looked down. "I'd probably go back to the ship."

"You wouldn't stay here?"

"Not if I had a choice. I don't feel like this is home."

"Then why did you come?"

"I came for you."

"Me?"

"Yes, you."

"Someone you think is a dead girl?"

"I don't really care what we are."

I looked at his dark eyes and long lashes, and got even more confused. I blinked away, staring out at the water. More people passed by and I thought about walking away, but he was like a magnet sitting next to me.

I'd seen several romance movies and read even more romance novels, and I hoped to one day feel like those characters. But not one single moment felt as powerful as the one I was in right now.

Everything felt like it was coming down to one decision in that moment.

"You know," I said, "my life has been turned upside down ever since you took my dad's shirt."

He put his elbows on his knees and ran his palm through his hair, looking at the ground. Everything I said was true and everything he said was insane, but he was sitting there, and the truth was, I wanted him to be there.

"So what next?" I asked.

"I don't know," he murmured.

"Well, we can't stay here forever."

He quickly raised his head and looked toward me. "So there is a we?"

"If this is my story, and I'm still sitting here, I'd say so."

He smiled a soft smile and put his arm around me, pulling me close. His defined muscles pushed back against me in all the right places, coming together like a puzzle. I rested my head on his shoulder, feeling an instant warmth.

"Are you sure?"

"Aren't you listening? Do you think I'd still be here after what you just told me if I wasn't?"

"What if it's my story?" he said.

"Either way, we're still here. So how does it end?"

"I have no idea," he said.

It was something I wanted to press, but something just came over me that was calm. And we sat there listening to the sounds of nature. I became one with it, accepting the beauty in how I felt. Once I let go of the questions and fear, a sense of acceptance came over me. After a while I squeezed his hand, knowing it was time to go. Even though I didn't know where.

"You ready?" I asked.

He nodded and stood first, pulling me into a hug. "Avery, I meant what I said. I would do anything for you. Always."

I gazed up in his eyes, and I saw everything I felt, right there.

"Same," I said.

He gave me a soft smile and a gentle kiss that told me we would be okay. We started walking down the beautiful path with flowers in bloom. I held his hand keeping close the memories of my mom and sister happy and that brought me joy. Then, we made the decision to focus only on the path ahead, wherever that took us.

Was it a story? Was it made up? I didn't know, but I knew one thing. I was really happy and felt more alive than any article could say I wasn't. How I felt at that moment was exactly like I wanted my life to feel.

About a quarter mile into our walk, the sun lit up so brightly, that we couldn't see the walkway. I pressed a little closer to him, feeling safer with my footing. We continued walking, our hands locked tightly and when the ray disappeared, it cleared the way to a path lined with people.

As we neared, I saw my father and my grandmother. J.P.'s parents exactly how I'd seen them in the book. His sister was also next to them, holding hands with a guy our age. They were all smiling and appeared to be waiting for us.

It wasn't a shocking moment, or even something we questioned. We just kept walking and they opened their arms to us, taking us in for a warm hug. The feeling of complete peace and unconditional love was exactly how I'd want my forever to begin.

I wouldn't be going home. I wouldn't be seeing my mom and my sister, but somehow that felt okay now. They would understand and maybe even smile from an unexpected inner peace if they could see me now.

More books by Shelena Shorts

The Pace

The Broken Lake(The Pace, #2)

The Iron Quill(The Pace, #3)

The Hour of Dreams(The Pace, #4)

The Syndicate

Gates of the Arctic

Visit

www.ShelenaShorts.com

www.ingramcontent.com/pod-product-compliance
Lightning Source LLC
Chambersburg PA
CBHW021642110726
47902CB00007B/1784